# RAMPAGE OF THE DROP BEARS

## BAZ GREENLAND

CANDY JAR BOOKS · CARDIFF
2022

Range Editor: Shaun Russell
Cover: Steve Beckett
Editorial: Will Rees & Keren Williams
Continuity Editor: Andy Frankham-Allen

ISBN: 978-1-915439-37-6

Printed and bound in the UK by
4edge, 22 Eldon Way, Hockley, Essex, SS5 4AD

Published by
Candy Jar Books, Mackintosh House
136 Newport Road, Cardiff, CF24 1DJ
www.candyjarbooks.co.uk

# PREVIOUSLY

As Matty stepped into the mass of vines, Lucy didn't really know what to say. He was leaving… forever. And so, presumably, she would be too. She knew that she'd never see him again. Although that made her sad, she was also looking forward to seeing Hobo. That's if he made it back OK. It now seemed like a long time since their adventure with Travers and Wells.

'Goodbye,' she whispered, smiling and lifting a hand to wave.

Movement in the corner of her eye suddenly caught her attention. There was a flower growing up out of the grass on the floor. *Oh no*, she thought, *Morai is trying to wipe my memory*. There was no way she was going to let that happen. She'd had quite enough amnesia to last a lifetime.

She spun to leave, only to find her way out of the bedroom blocked by more rapidly growing flowers.

She whipped her head from one direction to the other, but there were flowers growing everywhere. What could she do?

She held out her hand and stared at the ring, hoping that it would activate, willing it to take her home.

Pollen burst from the flowers, wafting through the air around her. She desperately held her breath, clutching a hand to her mouth and nose.

And then she felt it. The pull! The activation of the ring.

She was back in her room. Safe!

She took a deep breath, happy to be home. There was a funny smell. Floral.

'Oh no,' she whispered to herself, as she saw tiny particles floating around her room. The pollen had come with her. 'No, no, no, no, no. I can't lose my memories again.' She tried desperately not to inhale.

And now there were footsteps approaching. And a voice calling out. Her own voice… coming from just beyond her door.

'I'll be down in a minute!'

The time ring must have returned her to just before she had left. Lucy raced for the wardrobe, concealing herself among her clothes just as her earlier self entered the room. She heard the squeak of her bedsprings as the other Lucy sat down. She kept listening, trying to work out when exactly this was. She pushed the door a little, risking a peek. The other her was sitting on the end of her bed, an envelope in her hands. This was just before she had left.

The other her sniffed the air and gazed about. Lucy quickly pulled herself further into the wardrobe. And realisation hit her. The pollen! Her earlier self had breathed in some of the pollen that she had brought back. She had caused her own amnesia!

She blinked, her vision suddenly blurry. Her head felt funny.

The ring on her finger felt warm. It pulsed, almost as if it were alive.

She inhaled sharply.

Her head spun.

And once again she fell through the nothingness.

# CHAPTER ONE

# AN ENCOUNTER ON MENTONE STREET

Lucy Wilson landed with a thud, her hands reaching out and scratching against the hard paving stone beneath her. Her head was spinning, and her vision was blurry. She blinked, trying to adjust to her surroundings.

Where was she?

It was a busy street, full of people carrying shopping, cars racing by and all the sounds and bustle of a busy city. It was hot too. She could feel the beating sun on her back.

This place… it felt strangely familiar, like she had been here before. But it didn't feel like home either.

Where was home?

The sea?

She lived by the sea?

Her memories were foggy. Like a dream you

couldn't quite remember when you woke up. She had parents, and brothers, and a friend with no hair. And…

She didn't know their names, or what their faces looked like.

What was her name?

Lucy Wilson.

Yes, that was it. She was Lucy Wilson and she lived at…

…Somewhere by sea?

Lucy blinked. Those memories, they were all so scattered in her brain. She had the odd sensation that this had happened to her before.

She looked down at the ring on her finger. It was warm and pulsing slightly. Had she travelled through time?

Again?

Lucy took a deep breath and decided that she would have to go and investigate where she was. She got up with determination and took a step to her right…

…and almost walked straight into the boy on the bike!

Fred slammed the brakes on his BMX, steadying his feet on the ground to stop him from falling over the handlebars. The girl with the dark hair and skin fell against the wall next to them and slumped to the ground in a daze.

He gently rested the bike against the wall and reached out a hand to help her up.

'I'm so sorry, I didn't see you,' he said sheepishly.

He was met with a fierce glare as she stood up to face him. 'You should have been looking where you were going. Why were you riding your bike on the pavement anyway? You should have been on the road.'

He looked at her incredulously. 'On Mentone Street? Are you mad? Have you seen the traffic?'

The girl froze. 'Mentone Street?'

Fred nodded. 'Yes, we're on Mentone Street.'

'*This* is Mentone Street?'

Fred fought the urge to let out an exasperated sigh. After all, he was the one that had nearly run her down, so he couldn't get too cross.

She frowned. 'What city is this?'

'Melbourne.'

'And the year?'

How hard had she hit her head? 'It's 1985.'

The girl gasped. 'I'm back again!'

'Back where?' This time, it was his turn to frown. 'Where did you go?'

'Home, I guess,' she said with a sigh. 'Or at least, I think I did. I can't quite remember.' She gave him a deadly serious look. 'What is the date?'

Fred had a million questions, but it was probably

best to answer her question first. 'It's Saturday, the 21ˢᵗ September. Why?'

'Four weeks,' she muttered. 'Four weeks since Matty went back with Morai.'

*Matty?* This time, it was Fred who probably had the startled expression. 'You know Matty Franklin?'

'*You* know Matty Franklin?' she asked.

'That's what I just asked,' he replied haughtily. 'He's my best friend. Matty and his parents vanished a few weeks ago. I've been looking for them ever since.'

Fred pulled out the wad of papers from his backpack and handed one sheet to Lucy. It was the missing poster that he'd been putting up all over Mentone since the night his best friend had vanished. Seeing Matty's black and white photo, half of the only one they had ever taken together, filled him with sadness. He missed him terribly.

Lucy looked at the poster nervously. 'Err, I probably need to explain a few things.'

She rummaged in the pocket of her jeans and pulled out a laminated card.

'Are you Fred?'

'Yes,' he replied hesitantly.

She placed the card in his hand. It was a pass for Aussiecon Two. He was going to go to it the day after Matty disappeared. He remembered how excited Matty had been and couldn't help but frown at the thought of them not being able to get together.

But that wasn't what surprised him. It was his own face on the card. Why did she have his pass for Aussiecon Two?

'If this is Mentone Street, are we close to Space/Time Books?'

He blinked. There might have been a tear in his left eye, but he quickly brushed it away. 'Err, yes. It's just up the next street. I was going up there now to put some posters up. Matty and I, we went there all the time.'

'Great, let's go,' she said. 'Then I can give you all the answers you need.'

— CHAPTER TWO —

# TIME TRAVELLING ALIENS AND A GIRL FROM THE FUTURE

The moment Fred opened the door and led them into Space/Time Books, it all came flooding back to Lucy.

Matty being revealed as an alien prince, Jaria Dawn Thrice of the Aslante Separation, from fifty thousand years in the future.

Ashna, with the great coat, dark hair, and sunglasses.

The battle with the vines, helping Matty's royal guardian Morai and working with UNIT and Lieutenant Colonel Hardy.

And other memories too. The invisible woman. An adventure with HG Wells himself.

But her own life was still foggy. Her last trip to 1980s Australia was crystal clear in her mind, but she didn't know what her home life was like. She did remember that this has happened last time. It had taken a while for her memories to return.

Was it the side effects of using the time ring?

It was a strange feeling to be homesick when you didn't know who your family were, what your home looked like and how many friends you had. She was sure she had been able to remember some details when she arrived here, but even they were slipping away from her now.

Lucy assumed she had friends and family. She really hoped that someone was waiting for her, missing her. Wherever that place was, *whenever* it was, it certainly wasn't here.

Melbourne. Australia. 1985. A long, long time ago in a country far, far away. As Lucy walked into the science-fiction book store, she thought that sounded vaguely familiar. She'd seen that film. No, films. At least she knew she was from the future. The twenty-first century, perhaps?

Marvin was there to greet them behind the counter. He was tall and somewhat rotund, with a bright ginger goatee and bushy eyebrows. She had found him somewhat imposing the last time they had been here, but Matty had trusted him.

She would have to trust him too.

'G'day Fred,' he said. 'You can rest your bike over there.'

Fred nodded and set his bike against a space between two magazine racks. 'Hi, Marvin,' he said wearily.

'Any news on young Matty?' Marvin asked.

Lucy hesitated. Marvin didn't seem to be paying her the slightest bit of attention, despite the fact they had met before.

'Still looking,' Fred said, taking some of the posters from his rucksack. 'Would you be okay to put up a poster in the shop?'

Marvin took one poster and examined the photo. 'Of course,' he said. 'How are you holding up?'

'I miss him, I guess,' Fred sighed. 'Oh, this is…'

Lucy realised she hadn't given Fred her name. He looked at Marvin. 'I'm…'

'Not Fred's girlfriend?' Marvin interrupted with a smirk.

She hesitated. 'No, Lucy. As in, Lucy in the sky with diamonds?' she added, remembering how he had first referred to her the day she had arrived here in Space/Time Books.

Marvin frowned. 'Oh yes, like the song!'

'Yes,' she said with a sigh. 'You do remember me, don't you?'

'Erm, you're from Matty and Fred's book club, aren't you?'

Why didn't Marvin remember her? 'Yes,' she lied, hoping he would say something about

Aussiecon Two and their lengthy discussion on time travel. She had revealed to him that she was from the future, after all.

Maybe it was something to do with Morai wiping memories of Matty and his parents. It obviously hadn't worked completely, or Fred wouldn't be looking for him. But maybe Marvin had forgotten about their conversation at Aussiecon Two?

It was disappointing. Lucy had been hoping that he might help her work out why she was back in 1985 again.

She looked at Fred. 'Shall we chat upstairs?'

'Oh, sure,' he said, feigning excitement.

Lucy gave Marvin one more glance. 'Nice to meet you?'

The bookshop owner paused. 'Yes, nice to meet you too, Lucy in the sky with diamonds.'

The upstairs of Space/Time Books was just as she remembered. Rows of science-fiction books and a space to sit down and read. It was the place she had first met Matty. She realised she missed him a lot.

'I'm guessing you're as big a sci-fi geek as Matty?' she asked as she sat down.

Fred sat down next to her and scratched his head. 'Well, I like *Star Wars* and *Star Trek*. Matty is more into it than me. I'm more a history buff.'

'Well, that might come in handy.' Lucy sighed.

She realised her heart was pounding. Would he believe her when she told him the truth?

'Okay,' she muttered and took a deep breath. 'I need you to keep an open mind.'

'I can do that,' he replied hesitantly.

'Good. I know where Matty is. Or *when* he is. Do you know what happened at his house the night he disappeared?'

Fred frowned. 'No, I don't think so. His house?'

'You never went there?'

'I, I can't remember.'

'What about his parents?'

'Er, I can't remember. I mean, I remember school and the book club. And trips to the cinema and planning for Aussiecon Two. But, I don't remember even going to his house. Or meeting his parents. That's odd. I thought we lived close by.'

Lucy frowned. Morai wiping memories of Matty and his parents must have taken some of Fred's away.

'Matty was an alien.'

Fred looked at her and burst out laughing. 'That's hilarious!'

'I'm sorry, it's true. He wasn't really a human, though he didn't know it, of course.'

'Of course?'

'Well, I guess that's not that obvious. I mean, Matty didn't know until he met Ashna.'

'Who's Ashna?'

'His kidnapper.'

Fred's mouth opened wide. 'He was kidnapped?'

'Yes, from fifty thousand years in the future. He's actually a crown prince called Jaria Dawn Thrice of the Aslante Separation. I know this all sounds really crazy, but I don't know how to explain it more gently than that.'

'That *is* crazy!'

She sighed. 'I wish there was a way I could prove it to you. I know this hard to take in. I'm just…'

It suddenly hit Lucy that she was back in Australia, and she was all alone. There was no Matty this time. She had been ripped away from her family and she had no idea how to get home, wherever, *whenever* that was.

'Are you okay?' Fred asked.

She bit her lip, fighting back the tears. 'Not really. I… I don't have anywhere to go.'

'No family?'

'I don't know. I think I do,' she replied. Did she tell him she was a time traveller too? She wasn't sure he would believe her.

'Where do you live?'

'I… I was staying at Matty's house.' That was technically true, even if Matty's parents hadn't realised she was sleeping in the spare room. 'But now they've gone, I don't know what to do. Do you think there's a homeless shelter I can stay at?'

'You can't stay there!' Fred exclaimed. 'You can stay at mine. If you don't mind?'

Lucy smiled. She remembered that first trip on the Harris train, the day she arrived in Melbourne. She could see why Fred and Matty were friends. It seemed history was repeating itself.

'You're just like Matty.'

He grinned. 'We were best friends, after all. I can put you up in my basement, if that's all right?'

'It's better than a park bench.'

'Great!'

Her instincts told her she could trust him. 'I should also tell you, I'm a time traveller too.'

'A what now?'

Lucy sighed. 'Never mind.'

Fred was eying her suspiciously. 'Okay. Let's start again. 'Do you like movies?'

Lucy smiled with relief. She had been afraid he would think she was a lunatic and abandon her. 'Movies? I love them.'

'Fantastic! My parents own a video store. We can watch any film we want. More important question. Do you like popcorn?'

Lucy beamed. 'I love it!'

# CHAPTER THREE

# VIDEO NIGHT

Fred and Lucy walked into the video store that his parents owned. Brightly coloured movie characters adorned rows and rows of video covers, lit up by the neon lighting strips on the ceiling. Action movies, horror movies, comedy, romance and sci-fi; there was everything here you could want, all laid out in giant, glossy VHS tapes.

This was heaven for him. Picking a new favourite movie was as good as losing himself in a good piece of history in the local library. He had done a lot of both in the last few weeks since Matty had vanished. He really missed his best friend.

And now he had met Lucy. Who was this strange girl that had walked into him on Mentone Street, holding his pass from Aussiecon Two?

'What's good here?' Lucy asked, taking in the hundreds of VHS tapes on offer. 'I don't suppose you've got any good superhero movies?'

'Well, there's *Superman*, that's great,' Fred replied. He hesitated. 'I'm guessing there are lots of superhero movies where you come from, time traveller?'

'Yeah, they're massive. I'm trying to remember what else I like. There's a whole series of films about a boy wizard called… Harry something? I used to watch them with my brothers.'

'Your brothers?'

She hesitated. Her face looked incredibly sad. 'I think so. I can't really remember. I can't really remember much of anything.'

He didn't really understand what was going on. 'Come on, what are you after?' he asked, striding down between the rows of VHS tapes. 'Sci-fi, comedy or horror?'

Lucy crossed her arms. 'Are your parents really going to let you watch a horror movie?'

Fred looked at his father serving a customer at the counter and shrugged. 'Okay, what do you want to watch?'

'I don't know,' she muttered, looking at the cases. She looked sad.

Did she have family? Friends? Who was she?

On the train to Mentone, he had talked about how many times he had watched *The Empire Strikes Back* and *Return of the Jedi* with Matty. He had hoped she would tell him the real reason Matty was gone when he'd asked her again, but all she had done was talk about aliens and time travel.

He missed Matty, but he refused to believe he was some alien prince from the future. And there was absolutely no way he was believing that *she* was a time traveller. That was crazier than any of the stories he and Matty had read together.

Matty would have loved her stories. He would have believed her straight away. A time travelling girl from the future? Alien kidnappers? Either she believed all that nonsense and needed a head doctor, or she was hiding the truth from him. He just hoped he could get her to reveal what had really happened to Matty.

'Comedy perhaps?' Lucy asked.

All the films Lucy was looking at looked like rom-coms. His mum liked rom-coms. He hated them. They were all too predictable.

'What about something that's a little bit horror, a little bit comedy?'

'Nothing too scary,' she said nervously. 'Something your parents would let you watch.'

'*Gremlins*!' Fred exclaimed, grabbing the dark blue video box from a nearby shelf. A slimy green monster with a fluffy white stripe greeted him. That was Stipe. His favourite.

'Is it good?' she asked hesitantly.

'Is it good? Is it good? It's only one of the best

monster movies ever made. A boy, well a man really, gets a pet Mogwai for Christmas. It's a cute furry creature called Gizmo. But then it gets wet and has evil babies and then they feed other monsters and terrorise a small town on Christmas Eve. It's perfect!'

Lucy's eyes lit up. 'The three rules, right? Don't get them wet…'

'Don't expose them to bright light and don't feed them after midnight! You've seen it then?'

'I think there was one set in New York.' Lucy frowned. 'No, that was the sequel.'

Fred gave her an odd look. Gremlins in New York? Now that, he would pay to see.

'Yes, I think I have seen *Gremlins*. It was pretty scary, from what I can remember.'

'Maybe a little,' he conceded. 'But it's also only one of the best films of last year! That and *Ghostbusters*. And I'm sure *The Terminator* was great too but the parents, you know how parents are. They don't want to expose me to too much violence.' He rolled his eyes before continuing. 'Besides, if you *have* seen it before, maybe it will jog your memory.'

Lucy smiled. 'That's a good idea.'

'Fantastic!' he said excitedly. Time travelling nonsense or not, he really wanted to help her.

And what better way to do that than with *Gremlins* and a bowl of popcorn?

# CHAPTER FOUR

# FORGOTTEN MEMORIES

It was a short walk from the video store to Fred's house. It was dark outside, but streetlamps lit up the quiet streets of the neighbourhood. A few of the shops and houses they passed seemed familiar to her.

As they turned a corner, Lucy recognised a house a few doors down on the right. With a high green panelled fence and a mass of overgrown plants and grasses reaching all the way to the windows, it was just as she remembered, if maybe a little more overgrown.

Fred started to walk past the house, completely unaware that this belonged to Matty and his parents.

Lucy stopped by the garden gate.

Fred eventually noticed and began walking back down the pavement towards her. 'What's wrong?'

'Don't you recognise this house?'

He frowned. 'Why? Should I?'

'Matty lived here.'

Fred peered into the overgrown garden. 'It can't be. This place has been abandoned for at least a year.'

'Then where did Matty live?'

'I, I can't remember.'

'It's because memories of Matty and his parents were wiped when they returned to the future. He *is* an alien, I promise you.'

'And you're a time traveller?'

'Yes!'

'I'm not convinced,' Fred said, crossing his arms.

Lucy sighed with disgust. 'Matty believed me straight away when I told him I was from the future.'

Fred smirked. 'Yes, well he always was willing to accept crazy ideas. He loved sci-fi more than anyone I know.' He paused. 'Listen, I want to believe you, but there isn't any proof.'

Lucy shook her head. 'I really want to give you proof. But I don't know how. My memory of my own life, it's been wiped… by this time ring!'

She showed him the ring on her finger. 'The last time I arrived in 1985, I lost all my memories of my old life and it's happened again.'

'That sounds really frustrating.'

Lucy threw her arms up in the air. 'Tell me about it!'

'Okay, okay!' Fred laughed. 'Just given me some time to get my head around it, okay?'

She nodded. 'Okay.'

'Great. If you remember anything, you tell me. In the meantime, let's get to mine and watch *Gremlins*!'


Lucy slurped at the straw, feeling the bubbles from the lemonade tingle up her nose as she sat watching *Gremlins* with Fred. The plot seemed vaguely familiar, but she enjoyed it anyway. So far, the main character, Billy, has been given a cute Mogwai called Gizmo as a pet and Lucy had already fallen in love with him.

Naturally, Billy had forgotten the three rules. Gizmo had got wet, and now several evil Mogwai had eaten after midnight and transformed into gremlins. They had just watched the evil Mrs Deagle terrorised by Gremlins singing Christmas carols, and her malfunctioning stair lift sent rocketing off through a window. Fred laughed so hard, he had almost choked on his lemonade.

Lucy had to admit this movie was rather fun. But a vague sense of familiarity aside, it hadn't conjured up any memories yet.

Suddenly there was a knock on the staircase leading out of the basement and Fred's mum appeared, carrying a large bowl of popcorn. The smell filled the room and made her mouth water.

'Enjoying the movie?' she asked warmly.

Fred grinned as he walked up to grab the popcorn. 'Great, thanks! How's your boring romantic comedy?'

His mum laughed. 'It's not boring at all!' Just the one movie, okay? You both have school tomorrow.'

'Yes, Mum,' Fred groaned.

His mum ignored him. She was probably used to it. She looked at Lucy. 'Are you okay getting home on your own?'

Lucy nodded. Fred had told his mum that she was a mate from his class. She felt guilty that they were lying to Fred's parents and that he had set her up with a tent and blankets behind the sofa. At least she had a place to sleep tonight.

Fred's mum left and Fred returned to the sofa with the bowl of delicious-smelling popcorn. Lucy grabbed a handful and munched hungrily, enjoying the gremlins terrorising the town on screen.

'Can you imagine having to deal with that?' Fred asked, through a mouth full of popcorn. 'It would be so cool.'

Lucy swallowed hers. 'If gremlins attacked this town, I'm sure you'd be so scared, you'd wet yourself.'

Fred glared at her. 'No, I wouldn't. I'd take them all on.'

'Besides,' Lucy added, grabbing another handful of popcorn. 'The clean-up afterwards would be massive. I wouldn't want that job.'

The movie continued. The gremlins were lured into a cinema and were enjoying watching *Snow White and the Seven Dwarfs* when Billy, Gizmo and Kate blew them all up. Fred was convinced he could do it. Lucy informed him it was so dangerous, only someone in the movie could do something like that and survive.

Lucy had a flash of memory. She was sat on a sofa, not unlike this one, watching *Gremlins* singing along to Heigh-Ho and laughing uncontrollably with a boy next to her. She had laughed so hard, her sides hurt. The boy, who for some reason was completely bald, had laughed himself off the sofa.

Lucy looked down at the ring. It was warm and glowed ever so slightly.

'Fred, look!'

Fred paused the video. 'Look at what?'

Lucy showed him the glowing ring, but it had already stopped. 'It's, uh, nothing,' she muttered. 'Can you just give me a moment? I just need some air.'

Fred nodded and grabbed another handful of popcorn. 'Sure. You can use the basement door. Just push hard, the handle's a bit stiff.'

Lucy made her way into the back garden. It was very dark and cold. And the only sound was the rustling of wind in the trees around her. With the pitch darkness of a moon-less night, everything was rather spooky.

As she thought of that weird bald boy laughing and falling off the sofa, Lucy felt the faint heat on her hand as the ring glowed again. But this time, it wasn't just a small glow. The light grew brighter and brighter, so much that it lit up the garden around her and she was forced to shield her eyes.

And then the heat vanished, and the light was gone, and she was standing back in the cold garden in absolute darkness. Lucy felt her heart racing as she ran back inside, eager to tell Fred what had just happened.

Fred stared at her open mouthed. The TV was off, and the bowl of popcorn was empty. 'Where have you been?' he demanded.

Lucy frowned. 'I was just outside. Listen, I—'

'You've been gone over an hour!'

'What?'

'I was worried. I didn't know where you were, or if something had happened to you...'

Lucy looked at the worry in his face and felt more confused than ever. 'I was barely gone a minute. I...' She paused, looking down at the ring. 'Fred, I think something weird just happened.'

Fred folded his arms crossly. 'You're telling me.'

Lucy shook her head. 'No, you don't understand. To me, I've only just left. It was the ring. I had this memory of watching *Gremlins* with a friend—'

'A friend from back home?' asked Fred, interrupting.

Lucy nodded. 'Yes. When I thought about it, the ring glowed, and then there was this light. That's when I rushed back in to tell you.'

Fred frowned. He looked at his watch. 'You were gone for one hour and seven minutes, Lucy.'

'Maybe it's proof.'

'That you're a time traveller?'

'Yes. Maybe my memory of the future triggered the ring. Fred, I think I just travelled forward in time!'

# CHAPTER FIVE

# CLUES

The time ring was the only thing that could get Lucy home, and the only person with any possible knowledge of time travel, was Marvin. The owner of Space/Time Books had loads of knowledge and theories on time travel when she and Matty had revealed their secrets to him at Aussiecon Two. Even if his memories had been wiped by Morai, he was more likely to help her when she told him the truth.

Fred was less convinced, but he didn't have a better solution to her memory loss than going to see a 'head doctor'. She knew she wasn't crazy, and this wasn't amnesia. This was all the result of using the time ring.

They headed back to Space/Time Books the next day, and when they arrived, it seemed to Lucy that Marvin was waiting for them.

'Back so soon?' Marvin asked Fred, as they entered the store. 'Planning to start up your book group again?'

Fred looked at Marvin awkwardly as Lucy slunk in behind him. 'Oh, you know, couldn't wait. I've gotta buy one of those books now.'

Marvin grinned. 'Good for your soul. Good for my business too. Knock yourself out!' He looked at Lucy. 'Same for you, Lucy in the sky full of diamonds.'

She didn't really know how to ask Marvin about time travel, so she followed Fred upstairs and tried to think of the most natural way to reveal she was a time traveller. When she got to the top of the stairs, she saw Fred staring at the rows and rows of Polaroids on the back wall. Lucy was up there. Fred said he had a picture of himself on the wall too.

'Why does he do it?' Lucy asked.

'He says he likes to see the faces of everyone who comes to his store.' Fred replied, though he didn't sound convinced. 'It makes him feel grateful for every customer he gets.'

'It's creepy if you ask me.' Lucy shuddered. 'Maybe I should just tell him about the ring.'

'Your time ring?' Fred corrected her.

Lucy gave him a look. That wasn't him believing in her. He still thought she was crazy. 'Yes, my time ring.'

'Maybe it is best just to ask him.' Fred said. 'He might believe you're a time traveller.' He made a face.

But something told her there was more to Marvin than simply having his mind wiped. He seemed to remember Matty. So why not her? It wasn't as if Marvin was at the house with UNIT when Morai took Matty and his parents away.

'I just don't understand why he doesn't recognise me.'

'Time paradox? Is that a thing.'

'Unless he does, and he's pretending not to.'

Lucy began to pace the room. 'Marvin knew an awful lot about time travel,' she said cautiously. 'Maybe he has something here that can help us. If we find any clues, then we ask him.'

'I guess,' said Fred with a shrug.

'How much do you know about this place? Is there anything here beside books and magazines?'

'There's a back room, next to that bookcase.' Fred muttered, pointing across the room. 'I've seen Marvin go in there plenty of times. He *might* be hiding something in there that can help us.'

The tone of his voice suggested he was humouring her. 'Okay, let's take a look.'

'As long as we don't get caught.'

Lucy almost jumped as he heard the creak of footsteps on the stairs behind them. It was Marvin.

'Still trying to narrow it down?' he asked cheerfully, no hint that he knew what they were up to. Lucy wondered how much he had heard. But if he had, why didn't he say anything. There was something very suspicious about his behaviour. Lucy couldn't put her finger on it. It just felt like… instinct.'

'Check out *Ender's Game*,' Marvin said, taking a book off the shelf. 'New out this year. I think you'll like it.'

Fred's nodded. 'Yes, I saw that. I think you might be right.'

Marvin didn't move, but he seemed to be going out of his way not to look at Lucy. It was very peculiar indeed.

Fred took the book from Marvin and showed it to Lucy. The author was Orson Scott Card and the cover had a huge spaceship flying over a futuristic planet with a red moon in the distance. It reminded her of the sort of book Matty would have had in his bedroom.

'Would you mind if I read the first couple of pages to be sure?' Fred asked nervously.

Marvin nodded. 'You can even read the first chapter.' He gave them both a huge grin. 'But no more. They're for buying. It's not a library.'

Fred forced a laugh. 'Of course!'

As Marvin disappeared back downstairs, Lucy was even more convinced something was off with Marvin. 'Okay,' she whispered. 'Let's go.'

Fred put the book back on the shelf and they

walked over to a white painted door that led to the back room.

'Ready?' he asked Lucy nervously, putting his hand to the handle of the door.

She nodded, feeling a sense of panic. Why didn't she just ask Marvin? What was it about him that was stopping her?

The door opened and she followed Fred into the room beyond. Lucy could hear talking downstairs. There was no one to stop them. Taking a deep breath, she closed the door behind them.

The storeroom was nothing remarkable. A small room of white walls in need of a new paint job. There were a few cracks, a few cobwebs – she hoped they weren't the sort that came from Australia's more dangerous arachnids. The air was cold and stale, and the shelves were linked with cardboard boxes.

'Where do we start?' Lucy asked, peering into one of the open boxes.

Fred shrugged. 'I don't know. There's nothing here but boxes and more boxes. Not very exciting, is it?'

'Depends on what's in the boxes,' Lucy replied. 'Let's do some digging, shall we?'

They began their investigation, but quickly became apparent that there was nothing of interest. Most of the boxes were filled with copies of the same book, some others had bits of paper and stationery.

A few of the boxes were crammed with bits of old junk. It seemed this room was mostly a dumping ground for old rubbish, as much as it was storage.

Some of the boxes were sealed, but Lucy found an old pair of scissors and was able to cut through the tape to investigate the contents.

Just more books.

'Nothing!' Lucy said with an exasperated sigh, putting down the latest half-empty box.

'Hmmm,' pondered Fred. 'Maybe Marvin is just an ordinary guy that sells books after all?'

Perhaps he was. Perhaps he was just a guy that read a lot of science fiction and had lots of theories on time travel. But those Polaroids made her nervous. She had a flash of memory of holding one, looking at something scribbled on the back.

Unfinished business.

What was that about? Was Marvin involved? Could he be trusted?

'Just because he had a storeroom full of books in a bookstore, doesn't mean he wouldn't also have secrets hidden elsewhere. Those Polaroids… you have to admit, that's weird, right?'

'Maybe.'

'So, we keep looking?'

Fred frowned. 'But where? We can't exactly follow him home and break into his house?'

'Can't we?' Lucy asked excitedly.

She suspected Fred was trying to work out if she was joking. 'I don't know. Engaging in criminal activity feels a little bit of a leap at this stage.'

'So is sneaking in here.'

'Perhaps, but there's a difference between snooping in a storeroom and going through his personal belongings. Besides, I really don't want to go rooting through his underwear draw.'

'No, I don't want that either.' She shuddered. 'Okay, if not that, what?'

Fred thought about it a moment. 'When people are snooping around stores in the movies, they usually find a place to hide and then wait until the owner locks up and leaves them inside.'

'Won't your parents get suspicious when you don't go home for dinner?' Lucy replied. 'After all, if we're gonna get ourselves locked in, then that means we're here until at least 9.00am tomorrow.'

Fred looked at his watch 'Okay, maybe not. Why don't I just buy that book, so Marvin doesn't get suspicious, and then we'll work something out back at my house?

Lucy was about to agree when she spotted something off at the far wall opposite the door. 'What's that?' she asked, pointing to what looked like a long, fine crack in the paint that looked too straight to be natural.

Fred walked towards the crack and peered closer.

He gently ran her finger down the line on the wall. Suddenly there was a click and part of the wall slid back.

'It's a secret door!' he muttered in amazement.

There was another, smaller room beyond, but it looked nothing like the storeroom. It was almost pitch black, except for the glow of lights on a panel that lined a long, thin table. There was a small swivel stool and a contraption next to the panel of lights. It looked like a cross between a VHS player and a TV, with a round screen like a sort of TV panel. It could have belonged on the set of the USS Enterprise.

Lucy peered nervously inside, all her instincts being proven right. 'I knew there was something strange about him.'

'Marvin!'

Lucy had almost forgotten about the bookshop owner. Fred rushed back to the white door of the storeroom that led to the first floor. Lucy crept up beside him and held her breath as he turned the handle and peered outside.

There was no one by the bookshelves, but she could hear the creak of footsteps on the stairs.

Lucy looked at Fred in alarm. 'What do we do?'

Fred closed the door to the storeroom. 'This would be a really good time for your time ring to work.'

Lucy felt her heart racing again. 'You believe me?'

'Well, you were right about Marvin,' he whispered 'And if you really are telling the truth...

'I am!' she whispered back.

'Then prove it!'

There was the creak of footsteps outside. Marvin was coming!

Lucy looked at the ring on her finger nervously. How did it work? 'Where? Where do I go?'

'If Matty really is an alien, show me!'

The door handle began to turn. He had found them!

'Just do it!' Fred said, loudly and grabbed her wrist. 'Think about going somewhere else. The future. The past.'

'The past?'

'I don't know, just think!'

The door swung open just as Lucy's ring began to glow. There was a flash of white light, and everything changed...

— CHAPTER SIX —

# A TRIP TO SUBURBIA

'Where are we?'

It was night and they were stood at the end of a long street. It was cold too. Fred had a long-sleeved top on, but it wasn't thick enough to hold off the cold chill in the air.

'Well, we're not in Marvin's store anymore,' replied Lucy. 'I guess the real question is not where we are, but *when* we are?'

Fred gave her a hard stare. Something strange was definitely going on. But he wasn't convinced Lucy was telling him the truth. Or at least the whole truth.

Where were they? He didn't recognise this place. It could be any street in a big city at night. His parents didn't exactly let him wonder Melbourne alone in the dead of night. They could be two streets away from his house.

But that was impossible. They had just been in

Space/Time Books. With…

…with the strange room behind Marvin's storeroom. He had known the bookstore owner for at least two years now. Matty had introduced them when they set up their book club with Sally, Rob and Kyle. Or was it he that had introduced Matty to Marvin? For some reason, so many of his memories of his best friend seemed muddled these days.

He had no idea what was really going on in Marvin's bookstore or what those strange devices had been. All he knew was that he had been suddenly very afraid of getting caught and Lucy had done something with that ring on her finger.

'That doesn't prove it's a time ring,' he said defiantly. 'But I will admit that it moved us from one place to another.'

He looked around nervously, rubbing his cold arms. Was he trying to convince himself? Were her delusions about Matty being an alien and her being a time traveller all real?

He shook his head. 'No, as far as I am concerned, we are still in September 1985.'

'Then how do you explain what happened last night?' Lucy grumbled.

Fred shrugged. 'Maybe *you* just lost track of time.'

He could tell that he was irritating her, but he was also frustrated. Standing out on the cold street in the middle of the night, he just wanted to go home and watch a good movie.

Fred took another deep breath. He shouldn't take out his frustrations on Lucy. Whatever was really going on with her, she had nowhere else to go. 'I'm sorry,' he muttered.

Lucy glared at him. 'What? I didn't hear that.'

'Sorry!' he said a little more loudly.

Lucy's glare faded, and a big smile formed on her lips. 'Okay, let's just start over. Do you recognise this place?'

Fred looked up and down the street. It was obviously somewhere suburban. There were several large homes, fronted by gardens, lining the street. But looking down towards the light of the next streetlamp nearby, he saw a couple of larger buildings. Shops perhaps?

They began walking towards the large buildings. Disappointingly, they weren't that interesting. One looked like a storage facility, or maybe a factory. Large, shuttered doors were shut tight and there was nothing but darkness coming from the windows.

Fred and Lucy kept walking, heading past a few more houses until they found some shops. A bakery and a grocer, but both was closed. The only other light came from within the nearby houses, mostly from downstairs windows, behind curtains and shutters. It was early enough that no one was in bed, but late enough that shops and businesses had finished for the day.

Across the road, something caught Fred's eye. A small glint of light coming from within a grassy area between two houses. He grabbed Lucy's arm and pointed towards it.

That twinkle of light became a sphere of what he could only describe as a sizzling ball of electricity. It began to grow, almost as tall the buildings either side.

'What is it?' Fred gasped.

'Oh no,' Lucy sighed. 'I think it's aliens.'

Fred shook his head. 'That's stupid! Aliens aren't real, they're...'

He trailed off mid-sentence. The sphere of light became so bright that they had to shield their eyes. The whole street was lit up.

The surge of light faded and when Fred blinked, he saw something new where the sphere of electricity had been. A mass of withering green vines was in its place. They glowed in the light coming from of an upstairs window of one of the houses.

'Oh no, oh no!' Lucy muttered, grabbing Fred's arm. 'We need to go!'

'What is it?' he replied, his eyes wide. 'Are they aliens?'

'Yes, come on!'

But before he could move, the green vines began to wither and fade and in their place were two people. One was a tall woman in a grey coat. Her eyes glowed green, until they were hidden by a pair of sunglasses that she took from her coat pocket.

The other was a boy with glowing green eyes, Fred recognised that face.

It was Matty.

# CHAPTER SEVEN

# MATTY REALLY IS AN ALIEN

'What is happening?!'

Lucy grabbed his arm more and dragged him behind some bushes.

Fred crouched down beside her, peering through the leaves. Matty and the strange woman hadn't seen them, but they were looking up and down the street, searching for something.

'Do you believe me now?' Lucy hissed.

'I… I don't know…' Fred mumbled. His heart was racing, but he didn't know whether he was scared or excited. Maybe both.

The woman in the sunglasses touched something strapped to her wrist and placed a hand on Matty's forehead. The green glow in his eyes faded and he looked just as Fred remembered him. Maye a little smaller. He was sure Matty had been a few inches taller the last time he'd seen him.

Seeing his best friend, Fred felt the pain of

missing him. But his instincts told him not to run over and give Matty a hug.

The woman took Matty's hand and began leading him down the street. After a moment, Lucy began to move.

'Follow me and stick to this side of the road. If we keep our distance and use the trees and bushes for cover, we should be able to track them.'

Fred followed slowly. He wasn't used to tracking people. This wasn't the outback.

Almost as soon as they had started, Lucy froze, peering into an open bin. She rummaged inside.

'What are you doing?' he asked.

She pulled out a crumpled newspaper. 'Look at the date.'

Fred wrinkled his nose at the bad smell coming from within the paper and looked past the food stains splashed across the main picture. He read the date. 17th April 1984.

'It can't be,' he gasped. 'It must be a really old paper.'

Lucy chucked the paper back into the bin and rubbed her hands on the outside of her hoody. 'You think that newspaper had been sat on the top of that bin for over seventeen months? We've travelled through time, Fred.'

Fred wanted to argue, but it was hard to find a response that made any sense. Was she really telling the truth? Was Matty really an alien? The big electricity sphere, vines and glowing green eyes certainly suggested it. And Lucy was right about the newspaper.

'We're in 1984?'

Lucy nodded, a smile forming on her lips. 'That makes you a time traveller too.'

'Wow, Matty would have loved this!'

Lucy turned and stared up across the street. She grabbed his wrist. 'Come on! We're losing them!'

They could barely make out the strange woman and Matty further up the street, their figures silhouetted in the lights of a streetlamp. They hurried after them, keeping low behind a row of bushes.

Matty and the woman in the sunglasses seemed to have stopped. They were stood outside a restaurant. A man and a woman burst out of the entrance. They seemed to be arguing.

'Are they Matty's parents?' Fred asked. It was hard to make out faces clearly from across the street.

'Oh, this is it!'

Fred frowned. 'Is what?'

'They were supposed to die this night. Matty's parents. They were arguing when their car crashed. Ashna stopped that from happening, changed their memories and made them believe that Matty was their kid.'

'Who's Ashna?'

'The woman in the sunglasses. She kidnapped Matty from the future and brought him here.'

Sure enough, Matty's parents had exploded into a fully blown argument. He was calling her a nagging hag. She was telling him he didn't care about their relationship. Both were blaming each other for something that happened at Philippa and Jason's dinner party. They were clearly not happy.

Matty didn't seem to react at all. In fact, he looked like he was in a trance. The woman, Ashna, was focused on his parents, who had reached their car in the car park and were still arguing.

'Come on, let's get a little closer,' Lucy said, leading Fred to a nearby crossing.

When they reached the other side of the road, they began walking quickly back towards the restaurant.

'Who is this Ashna?' Fred asked.

'She's pretending to be Matty – Prince Jaria Dawn's royal guardian. Or at least, that's what she tells me and Matty at Aussincon Two. She's actually his kidnapper. She's working for… oh what's it called, the Lainor Dusk Septance? And she wears a Chloro-sym interface on her wrist. We have to be careful. She uses it to control plants.'

'Maybe I should demand a shrubbery,' Fred said with a smirk.

'What?'

'I guess you've never seen *Monty Python and the Holy Grail*?'

Lucy gave him a blank look and they hurried on. He didn't really understand what was going on, but it was definitely both exciting *and* scary.

They reached the restaurant and navigated their way quietly towards the edge of the car park. They snuck down behind a low wall, watching as Ashna walked up to Matty's parents.

'No, I've had enough!' Matty's mum screamed.

'You've had enough? *You've* had enough?' Matty's father screamed back.

It was all rather upsetting to watch. They were so focused on shouting at each other that they didn't see the woman in the sunglasses until she was right behind them.

Ashna muttered something and Matty's parents collapsed into her arms. Fred and Lucy watched as she opened the car door and placed their unconscious bodies in the front seats.

Matty was still stood on his own in a complete trance. Fred was worried about him.

'I should help him,' he said, getting up from behind the wall.

'No!' Lucy snapped. 'This is supposed to happen!'

'But you said this Ashna was his kidnapper. We can't just leave him with her.'

Fred climbed over the wall and began running towards his friend.

'Stop!' Lucy cried, climbing over the wall after him.

There was a slam of a car door and Fred froze. Ashna was staring at him from across the car park.

She removed her sunglasses, revealing the glowing green swirl of light where her eyes should be.

Fred's blood went cold. He looked at his friend, standing in a trance and then back to the woman.

'Who are you?' she demanded.

Before he could respond, Fred felt himself being pulled back by Lucy.

'Come on! We've got to go!'

'But Matty!'

'He'll be okay. Come on. Fred! We have to run!'

## — CHAPTER EIGHT —

# ESCAPE!

Lucy ran. She wasn't even sure Ashna was behind them as she charged down the street, her feet pounding against the pavement with each leap. Fred was panting furiously at her side.

They had completely bypassed the crossing and were racing down the busy street, looking for a way to escape. She knew how dangerous Ashna was and she didn't want to get caught.

Not to mention what an encounter with the alien kidnapper would do to the timeline. Fred had never met her, but she had. If Ashna knew who Lucy was in 1985, things might turn out very differently.

Unable to run any further, they stopped to catch their breaths.

Across the road from them, tall iron gates rose majestically into the night. At either side was a long, high brick wall with trees clearly visible beyond them.

Fred pointed at the gate. 'Let's! Go! In! There!' he panted. 'We. Can. Hide. From. Her.'

'Agreed!' Lucy gasped.

Fortunately, there wasn't much traffic to slow them down. Looking both ways, they walked across the street. The gate was huge. Wrought out of iron and fashioned into swirling patterns, there were certainly plenty of footholds they could grab and climb onto.

There was a big sign on the front of the gate.

## THE MELBOURNE KOALA SANCTUARY

Lucy had never seen a koala in real life, but they always looked like cute teddy bears. Even so, she wasn't sure sneaking into the sanctuary and disturbing them would be the most wise option.

'Maybe we should find somewhere else?' she began nervously.

'You two!'

She turned and saw Ashna across the street. She was wearing the sunglasses again and she looked very angry.

There was no time to waste. They began climbing the gate, grabbing hold of the metal rungs, hoisting themselves up as high as they could go. Frantically, they hoisted themselves over the top of the gate and clambered down the other side. Her hands and feet hurt, but she could handle a little discomfort if it meant they got to safety.

As they jumped down to the ground inside the entrance, Fred came face-to-face with the Ashna through the gate. She looked at Fred with a curious gaze.

Lucy held back in the shadows, afraid of being spotted.

Ashna reached through the gate to grab him. Fred stepped back and broke into a run with Lucy, charging into the darkness, away from the gate and the alien assassin that had almost caught them.

Lucy could barely see anything. There were no lights, except for the glow of a nearby ticket booth. A couple of confectionary stands, and a gift shop, were closed, and there was no one around to stop them. She presumed the koala sanctuary didn't get many people breaking in at night.

Ashna was still standing at the gate, watching them and Lucy was glad that they were concealed by darkness. Still, she decided they had better hide, in case Ashna climbed over and followed them in. She led Fred around the back of the ticket booth and saw a light ahead. It was a single-story building and the illuminated sign above it read: Office and Security.

So, there might be someone here after all. Not waiting to find out, they took a path away from the building, heading deeper into the sanctuary.

They wandered for a few minutes, turning off the path and moving into the trees. It was warmer, without the night chill on their faces. The rustling of leaves in the trees above them was oddly soothing. Still, they had to move slowly and carefully. They could barely see their own feet on the ground beneath them.

When they were certain they weren't being followed, they dared to rest. They were a long way from the entrance now, so there was no way to check if Ashna had followed them. Lucy hoped she had returned to her mission of saving Matty's parents and placing him with them.

It had been strange to see Matty again, looking a little younger than she remembered. She wished she could have done something, but the damage was already done. He had already been kidnapped by Ashna. At least now he was going to enjoy a year of life in Australia, discovering sci-fi books and films and forming a book club with best friend Fred.

Matty's best friend was very quiet. He was probably adjusting to everything he had just witnessed.

'Do you think we might see any koalas?' Lucy asked quietly, sitting on the soft, grassy ground.

Fred sat down beside her, more a shadow than a real person in the darkness. 'I assume we will. This is the biggest koala sanctuary this far south, from what I remember. My parents brought me here once.'

Lucy wondered what her own parents were like. She wished she could remember more details about her life. She hoped her parents were alive, wherever and *whenever* they were.

'Why did we come here?' Fred asked.

Lucy frowned. 'The koala sanctuary? You suggested it.'

'No, I mean 1984.'

'Oh, I don't know.'

Lucy looked down at the time ring. 'I can't remember how it works. There aren't any buttons. It just… senses where I need to go, I guess.'

'And it sensed you needed to come here?'

'Maybe. You suggested we go to the past.'

'Well, I was desperate! I didn't really believe it would work.'

'Well, it did.'

Fred sighed. 'That still doesn't explain why we came *here*?'

Lucy thought about it a moment. 'Maybe it was so I could give you proof.'

Fred laughed. 'Well, I guess you've proved yourself now.'

'You believe me?'

Fred seemed to think about it for a moment. 'There's a lot that doesn't make sense to me. But I think I do.'

Lucy felt a surge of relief. She was grateful that Fred had helped her and given her a place to stay, but having someone who believed in her fantastical adventures made her feel safer somehow.

'Thank you,' she said with a smile.

Fred frowned. 'For what?'

'For not running away the moment you first met me.'

Fred laughed again. 'I guess it was destiny.'

Lucy laughed with him. 'I guess it was.'

# CHAPTER NINE

# LEGEND OF THE DROP BEARS

Lucy and Fred wandered through the sanctuary, looking for a way out.

They didn't return to the main gate. Ashna might be waiting for them and there still might be a security guard, who wouldn't take too kindly to finding them inside after opening hours. Fred suggested they find a back way out of the sanctuary. There had to be one, for fire safety purposes. Lucy thought it was a good idea and they ventured deeper in.

They found a small, tarmacked path, and a sign that pointed to some nearby toilets in one direction and the gift shop the other. The gift shop was obviously near the entrance, so they decided to go the other way. Eventually, they came to a high back wall, but there was no sign of an exit.

They were turning back on the path, when they

saw a glow of light and a man with a torch walking towards them. Quietly, Lucy and Fred slunk into the trees and watched as the man passed them by. He wore a pale grey uniform and whistled as he walked by. It was obviously a security guard, out on patrol.

Luckily, he hadn't noticed them.

'This way,' Fred said, grabbing Lucy's wrist and leading her into the trees. 'Let's keep to this side of the sanctuary. There has to be a back entrance somewhere.'

Lucy followed, feeling a little less certain. It was very dark in those trees, even with the white, ghostly glow of the moon that had peered through the clouds above them.

'What if there are poisonous spiders in there?' she asked nervously. She knew a bite from a spider in Australia could be far more deadly than any back home in the UK. It was odd how certain she was on particular facts, when others, like her whole entire family, were out of reach.

'Relax, there's no dangerous spiders here,' Fred said, but she wasn't that reassured.

They wandered through the trees and found the back wall a second time. Again, there was no sign of an exit and it was too high to climb. Lucy was getting very cold now, and hungry. She wished she had a coat to wear over her hoody.

Finally, they came to a stop in a secluded glade

where the moon lit up the grassy ground. It was all rather pretty, but she would have enjoyed it more if she knew how to get out of this place.

'We haven't seen a single koala bear,' Lucy said with a sigh, as she sat down on the ground and rubbed her cold arms furiously.

'Maybe they're all asleep?' Fred suggested, sitting down next to her, and taking out something from his pocket. It was a small packet of biscuits, slightly broken. He handed her one. 'Hungry?'

'How did you...?' she began, confused.

'Always be prepared for any situation!' he said with a grin.

Lucy took two biscuits and munched hungrily. It felt good to eat something.

Lucy looked up into the branches of the trees above them. Bathed in moonlight, she could see them quite clearly. Leaves danced in the wind, branches swayed, but they were otherwise empty.

'Don't they sleep in trees?' Lucy asked. She was disappointed that she hadn't seen a single koala. They must have been in the sanctuary a good hour or two by now.

Suddenly there was a loud crack of a branch nearby. It was so loud, it made her jump out of her skin.

'You okay?' Fred asked.

Lucy nodded. 'Just a little startled, that's all.

Koalas, they're pretty tame, aren't they? They're not likely to attack us for being in their territory?'

'They are mostly harmless,' Fred assured her. 'Unless, of course, they're drop bears.'

Lucy frowned. What was a drop bear?

'Drop bears… they're something of a legend here in Australia.'

'What are they?'

Fred leaned a little closer, his face pale in the moonlight. He looked like he was going to tell her a ghost story. 'Evil koala bears.'

She looked at him in alarm, her heart racing. 'Evil koala bears?'

'Yes, they hide in the trees and when you least suspect, they drop onto your head and attack you!'

Lucy looked up nervously at the branches above her.

'That's why they're called drop bears,' Fred continued, his voice lowered in an almost menacing tone.

'I don't like the sound of them.' Lucy shuddered.

Fred leaned back. 'It's okay. As I said, they're just a myth. Something the locals tell tourists to scare them.' He paused. 'In fact, they're a lot like gremlins in that matter. There are even three rules.'

Lucy swallowed hard. 'Three rules?'

'Yes. Follow them and you'll be safe.'

Lucy waited for Fred to tell her and when he

didn't, she had to take a deep breath to calm herself. She was obviously more afraid than she had realised. And tired. Her imagination always ran away from her when she was tired.

'Okay then, what are they?'

Fred took a big, dramatic breath for effect. 'Slather yourself in Vegemite, speak in an Australian accent, and call everyone Bruce!'

Lucy frowned and then she laughed. A deep belly laugh, so big, it hurt her sides. 'Bruce? Really?'

Fred held up his arms defensively. 'Hey, as I said, it's just an urban legend. I didn't make up the rules!'

She felt a lot more relaxed. 'Like I'm going to smother myself in Vegemite? I don't even like it on toast!' Of course, it was called Marmite where she came from. Another fact she knew with absolute certainty.

There was another loud snap. Lucy stood up quickly and grabbed Fred's hand.

'Worried it's a drop bear?' he asked with a smirk.

'Of course not!' she replied with a glare. 'Doesn't mean it isn't dangerous though.'

'Come on, let's keep searching.' Fred said, leading her out of the small glade.

There was another snap. This time in a different direction and a rustling in the trees that sounded like more than just the wind. Were the koala bears waking up?

Or worse still, what if it was Ashna? Her chloro-sym interface could control plants. What if she had commanded whole trees to attack them?

As they hurried back to the wall, something landed with a thud behind them. Lucy couldn't make anything out in the darkness, but a sudden scurrying among the undergrowth unnerved her.

'There is definitely something in here with us.' she whispered.

'Maybe a koala fell out of a tree?' Fred suggested. 'Maybe we disturbed it in its sleep?'

'Or it's a drop bear,' Lucy tried to make a joke.

As she peered into the darkness of the trees, she felt as if something was watching her. Not just one something either.

Another crack of wood echoed behind them. Then a second and a third, all from different directions. Were they surrounded?

'I want to go home!' She sighed and suddenly there was a faint heat as the time ring on her finger began to glow.

Without hesitation, she grabbed Fred's hand and in that brief moment before the flash of white light took them away, she saw movement in the trees. Something was coming towards them.

They barely escaped in time.

# CHAPTER TEN

# TROUBLE IN THE PAPERS

Fred scooped a massive spoonful of Froot Loops into his mouth, enjoying the taste of the crunchy, fruity goodness, before he swallowed. He barely paused for breath before spooning up another, milk sloshing over the side of his mouth as he lifted the spoon to his lips. He had more important things to do than sit here having breakfast.

'Slow down, Fred!' Mum said, with a long, steady stare. He avoided those eyes. He knew he had no chance of winning a staring contest with her.

He crunched and swallowed. 'Sorry, got things to do!'

'Well, I think it's important to share breakfast together. You've had most of your meals in the den lately. At least I know you're eating well, the portions you take with you.'

'He's a growing lad,' Dad added.

The large portions he took with him had nothing to do with being a growing lad. He had to take double portions of everything, so that he could give half to Lucy. His parents still had no idea his 'friend from down the street' was living in the basement. Fred wasn't sure if he and Lucy were being clever and sneaky, or his parents were just that dumb. Maybe it was a mixture of both.

'All I ask, is to enjoy breakfast and dinner together,' Mum added, taking a sip of her morning coffee. She smiled with satisfaction. She was constantly telling him it was the rocket fuel she needed to get through the day.

Fred kept eating in silence, slowing down just a little, and feeling a little guilty too. After everything Lucy had told him about Matty's parents, and seeing just how unhappy they had been too, perhaps spending a little bit of time with them wasn't so bad after all.

Dad was half-engrossed in the newspaper, his coffee untouched, his toast half-eaten. Somehow, he wasn't getting told off.

'Hmmm, load of nonsense if you ask me.'

'What, dear?' asked Mum.

'Some locals with half a brain, claiming they were attacked by a bear last night.'

'A bear?'

Fred frowned. 'There aren't any wild bears in

Australia.'

'Except koalas,' Mum added.

Dad laughed. 'Well, that's just it. This lunatic claims a koala bear fell out a tree and bit him. Honestly! The rubbish they print these days!'

Fred swallowed. 'They *are* just myths, aren't they?' he asked nervously.

Dad put down the paper, a bemused smile on his face. 'Koalas?'

'No, drop bears?'

'Well, of course they are, Fred!'

His mum sighed. 'Honestly, Bradley. I told you not to go telling him ghost stories.'

'It's not a ghost story,' Dad replied. 'Anyway, it's just a thing the locals make up. Like the Loch Ness Monster in Scotland. Or the Yeti. They're not real.'

'The Loch Ness Monster isn't real?' Fred was convinced that it was some kind of prehistoric dinosaur that had settled in one of Scotland's big lakes.

'No, I'm afraid not,' Dad said with a smile. 'Listen, it's probably just a koala that fell asleep. Or maybe the man in the report was drunk. Who knows? Maybe someone dropped a teddy bear on his head to scare him.'

'Maybe,' Fred said, rising from the table and grabbing a slice of buttered toast. 'Mind if I eat this downstairs?'

'If you must,' Mum said with a sigh.

Fred took that as a yes, and rushed down to the basement, where Lucy was waiting for him. He knocked three times on the banister to let her know it was safe to come out.

'Sorry, it's a bit cold,' he said, handing her the toast.

'It's fine, thanks,' she replied, taking a bite hungrily. 'Everything okay upstairs?'

'Yeah. Mum just wanted a *family* breakfast.'

He sat down on the small sofa, pondering the report in the paper as he waited for Lucy to finish her toast. It didn't take her long.

'What do you think it was in that koala sanctuary?' he asked her nervously.

Lucy frowned. 'I thought you said it was just our imagination and a bit of wind?'

Fred wondered if he should tell Lucy about the newspaper report, but she already had enough on her mind. Like trying to use the time ring. She had spent every moment of the last two days, trying to find out how it worked.

Lucy had told the time ring to take her home. To take her back one week. And more crazy things – like the moon landing, and an event she vaguely remembered somewhere in the back of her mind called *To An Unsung Hero*, even though she had no idea what it meant.

But nothing ever happened. She shook her hand. She tapped the ring. She even tried jumping up and down and spinning around. But nothing she did worked.

Lucy brushed toast crumbs off her cheek and sat down next to Fred. 'You okay?'

Fred nodded, though his mind was elsewhere. *A koala dropped out of a tree and attacked a man? Wasn't that* exactly *what a drop bear did*? he thought.

'…so of course, that's what I think we'll need to do.'

Fred blinked. 'Sorry?'

'Were you even listening?' Lucy demanded with a sharp look.

He smiled sheepishly. 'Sorry, no I wasn't.'

Lucy's look softened. 'Okay, let's get out of here. It's Saturday. I've run out of ideas with this ring. You obviously have something troubling you. Why don't we go out and clear our heads a bit?'

Fred smiled. 'That sounds like a great idea.'

Lucy snuck out through the basement door and went round to the front, pretending she had just arrived to ask Fred to go and hang out. She came back down to the basement and waited, while he grabbed his backpack of supplies. His mum even made sandwiches for them both and gave them a small tin of fruit cake slices and some fizzy pop. At least this time, she knew she was feeding Lucy.

They took the train into the centre of Melbourne and hung out in an arcade, playing Pacman and Space Raiders. It was good to distract himself with something other than drop bears, alien kidnappers and time travel. The sun was out, and the temperature was hot, so they headed down to a park Fred knew where they could sit at the edge of a stream, dangling their feet in the water as they sat on the grassy bank, munching their sandwiches and drinking their pop. It was a pleasant way to spend their Saturday lunchtime.

They decided to save the cake for later, dried their feet and headed back out of the park in search of a joke shop Fred had once found. It wasn't far from Space/Time Books, but they decided it was best to avoid Marvin for as long as possible. They still had all those unanswered questions about the secret room in the back of his shop and he hadn't gone back to pick up his other rucksack yet.

They were just turning onto the street with the joke shop when something caught Fred's eye. It was a newspaper headline, bold and clear as day on the front of a newspaper stand.

**Are drop bears real and
are they here in Melbourne?**

Lucy froze beside Fred, her mouth open, her eyes wide. 'Drop bears? You said they weren't real?'

'They aren't,' Fred replied, though he didn't think he sounded convincing.

It was a different newspaper than the one Dad had read. Two newspapers writing about a fake, Australian legend?

Fred bought a copy of the paper and they rushed to the nearest bench to read the article. A man in his thirties had been attacked travelling home from work last night. A feral koala, the size of a dog, had jumped out of the tree and bit him on his shoulder. While his injuries weren't severe, he was in hospital for observation, and the RSPCA had been called in to track the wild animal.

'Well, there you go then,' Lucy said, pointing to the man's description of the Drop Bear being the size of a dog. 'Koalas aren't that big, so it can't have been a Drop Bear.'

'Also, they're not real,' Fred added.

Lucy smirked. 'Yes, there is that. It must be something else. Look, the article says the man had just left a bar after work. He was probably drunk.'

'That's what my dad said.'

Lucy frowned. 'Your dad?'

Fred looked at her sheepishly. 'My dad was reading about it at breakfast this morning. His paper had said a bear had attacked a man by dropping out of a tree and biting him.'

Rather than react angrily, Lucy laid a reassuring hand on his shoulder. 'Is that what was on your mind earlier?'

'I didn't want to worry you. After what happened in the sanctuary and with this time ring to deal with...'

'Promise me you won't keep anything from me?'

'I promise.'

There wasn't anything substantial on the front page article. But there was a link to another article on page eight.

**Where does the myth of drop bears come from?**

With excitement, Fred turned to page eight and read the article aloud.

'Are drop bears a myth? We all know they are. Killer koala bears that drop out of tress and attack people are merely a joke played on tourists. The truth is, Australia has its own share of dangerous wildlife, without killer bears thrown into the mix.

'But where does the myth come from? Ignoring the three rules – speak in an Australian accent, smother yourself in Vegemite and call everyone Bruce, which is obviously all part of the joke played on unsuspecting tourists – there may be an historical context to these legends, and it goes all the way back to the Pleistocene period.

'The Thylacoleo carnifex, also known as the "marsupial lion", is an extinct species of carnivorous marsupial mammal that lived in Australia, until its extinction 46,000 years ago. With its powerfully built jaws and strong forelimbs and retractable claws, it was certainly a fierce predator. And how does it relate to the terrifying Drop Bear? Well, maybe that's all down to an old native rock painting that seems to show a Thylacoleo standing on a tree branch. The truth is, even if drop bears were real, you'll have to go back almost a million years to find one.'

'I don't think it has anything to do with what we saw in the sanctuary,' Lucy said with a sigh. 'It would have eaten us if it was there.'

He put the newspaper in his backpack and stood up. 'I've got an idea. Let's go and see a Thylacoleo carnifex.'

'How?'

'There's a museum of natural history near here. It's got loads of old prehistoric skeletons.'

Lucy grinned. 'They got a T-Rex?'

'I'm fairly certain they do.'

Melbourne Museum was the largest museum in Australia. Fred could spend days in there, getting lost among the dinosaur bones, ancient artefacts, treasures, and tombs.

For Lucy, it was the dinosaurs that excited her the most. She had a vague memory of a museum in London, with giant dinosaur bones and an animatronic T-Rex. She thought she had been there with an older brother… and his husband? Which was confusing. Fred was fairly certain men couldn't marry other men. Maybe the future was more enlightened.

It was a very big museum, and it took them a while to find a skeleton of a Thylacoleo Carnifex. The description of the placard on display said it was from the early to the late Pleistocene period, that had lived somewhere between 1.6 million and 35 thousand years ago.

There were other ancient Australian Megafauna too, including a Diprotodon, which was a kind of giant wombat and a Procoptodon Goliah, the largest-known kangaroo to have ever lived.

The most surprising thing about the Pleistocene display were the models of ancient aboriginals. Fred hadn't realised that humans had lived alongside the terrifying Thylacoleo Carnifex, maybe even hunted it. The idea of something this size jumping out of a tree and attacking you, was enough to make his blood run cold.

'Fifteen minutes until the museum closes. Please finish up and make your way to the main exit,' a shrill, female voice announced over the loudspeakers.

'I wish we had more time to study this,' Fred said wearily, looking up at the prised jaws of the Thylacoleo Carnifex skeleton.

'Me too,' Lucy replied. 'Maybe we can come back next weekend, if we haven't had any luck with the ring by then.'

'Sure.'

'Do you think there is something here?' Lucy added nervously. 'A connection between this creature and the attack in the newspaper?'

Fred shrugged. 'I don't see how. More people would be talking about it if one of these was walking around Melbourne.'

'I guess.' Lucy sighed. 'I just wish...'

She froze. Fred saw why. The time ring was startling to glow.

Lucy grabbed his hand. In a flash of light, the museum around them vanished...

...And in its place, a suffocating heat.

Fred shielded his eyes from the intense glow of the sun above them. The heat was so powerful, he could already feel his body getting drenched in sweat. Before them, a desert stretched out for miles.

He turned to Lucy. 'I don't think we're in Melbourne anymore...'

# CHAPTER ELEVEN

# A PLEISTOCENE SAFARI

Lucy couldn't breathe. She had just got used to the Australian heat, but this was something else altogether. Her whole body was soaked with sweat. She quickly removed her hoody and put it in Fred's rucksack and rolled the sleeves of her t-shirt over her shoulders, hoping it would cool her down. It did nothing. If anything, the intensity of the sun on her bare arms only made her hotter.

'Where are we?' She gasped, as she stared out across the desert.

Fred was right. They weren't in Melbourne anymore. Apart from the occasional shrubbery in the sand, there was no sign of life anywhere. She stared down at the ring. It was no longer glowing, but she still felt a kind of tingling sensation on her finger. Where had it taken them?

'*When* are we, more like,' Fred replied. He was

getting used to this time travel stuff.

Fred grabbed two caps from his rucksack, and handed one to Lucy. She was glad to have something to shield her face and even happier when he retrieved a bottle of pop from the bag. His mum must have packed extra.

The bottle fizzed as he twisted the cap. He passed it to her for the first drink. While a little warm, the fizzy liquid felt good as it ran down her dry mouth and throat. He took it back, had a swig, and returned it to the pack.

'Are we in a different part of Australia, or is this the past?' Lucy asked nervously. She knew the answer. It was both.

'What were you thinking just before we left the museum?' he replied hesitantly.

Lucy remembered looking at the large skeleton of the Thylacoleo Carnifex. 'I was wondering if there was a connection...'

'...with the drop bears?'

'Yes.' Lucy hesitated. 'I was wondering if there might be such a thing as a Thylacoleo Carnifex still living in 1985. And I—'

'You what?'

'I thought, if we could see one, for real, it might help us understand the connection with the reports in the papers.'

'Do you think the time ring took us back to the

Pleistocene Period?'

Lucy wanted to laugh at such a ludicrous suggestion, but she had the sneaking suspicion he might be right. 'To see a Thylacoleo Carnifex?'

'I think we should try and find some shelter from the sun.'

That wasn't a bad suggestion. Even when Fred found half a bottle of sunscreen in his pack, she suspected it would offer little protection from the intensity of the sun beating down on them. With another swig of pop, they began trekking across the dusty desert plain, hoping that they might find somewhere to shelter.

It didn't take long to find a rocky outcrop in the distance. There were no birds in the sky, but vegetation became more frequent, the closer they got to the rocks. A few spindly trees, half-dead in the dirt, and some outcrops of grass. Lucy guessed there had to be water nearby. Maybe even a cave, if they were lucky.

Something stirred in the distance, a cloud of dust blowing into the brilliant blue sky.

'What's that?' Fred asked.

Lucy tried to make out what the shadowy figures were, moving across the desert. Luckily for them, they weren't heading directly in their direction. Lucy had no desire to be someone's dinner.

'They look like... ostriches,' she replied. The

giant, wing-less birds, running across the sand, reminded her of geese, only much, much bigger.

'I think I saw them in the museum,' Fred said, rummaging through his backpack and taking out a leaflet he'd picked up in the exhibit. 'Yes, they're Genyornis Newtoni.'

'Are they carnivorous?' she asked nervously.

Fred shook his head. 'No, like most birds in the Pleistocene Period, they're herbivores. Plant eaters.'

'Well, that's a relief,' she replied.

The three birds ran past them. Despite having no idea why they were here, Lucy felt a sense of wonder at seeing something that was extinct back in the twentieth – and twenty-first century.

'I wonder if we'll find any other creatures,' Fred said, before taking another swig of pop and handing her the bottle.

She took a long gulp and returned the cap. 'As long as they're all herbivores.'

Fred looked at her nervously. 'Well, there's no sign of a Thylacoleo Carnifex yet.'

Yet. She handed him the almost empty bottle. 'Come on, let's get to those rocks.'

It didn't take long to reach the rocks. By now, Lucy's clothes were soaked with sweat and her skin felt extremely hot to touch. Fred looked even worse than her.

There was no shelter to be found, but the biggest

outcrop of rocks ahead looked much higher. There were even a few trees around and they managed to find one with enough foliage to give them a moment of shade from the sun.

As they huddled under the branches, there was a low rumbling coming from nearby.

From behind a row of bushes, a huge hippopotamus-liked creature emerged. It was at least a couple of metres long, and it reminded her of wombats she had seen in Australia. It lumbered forward, and chewed hungrily at a bush, consuming most of its leaves in one bite. Lucy stared at it in amazement.

'Have you seen the size of that thing!' Fred said with a gasp, taking out his leaflet.

He scanned the images, looking for the creature.

'Ah, here it is!' Fred cried. 'The Diprotodon is the largest known marsupial to have ever existed and was native to Australia during the Pleistocene Period, from about one point six million years ago until its extinction some forty-four thousand years ago.'

'Well, I guess we know when we are, give or take a few thousand years.' Lucy grinned. Despite the suffocating heat and the terror of wondering if they would ever get back, she had to admit that this was pretty amazing.

They watched in awe as the Diprotodon attacked

a second bush with it's huge, two-toothed jaw.

'This is a proper Pleistocene safari!' Fred exclaimed with joy.

'It's pretty special,' she admitted. 'We'll be the only ones to have done this.'

'Except other time travellers perhaps.'

'Maybe.'

They finished off the pop and ate a little bit of Fred's mum's fruit cake as the Diprotodon continued its lunch. There was something odd about sitting under a tree on the edge of a desert, eating cake and watching a species that died out a million years ago.

But it was all very exciting too.

Lucy had the feeling that her life had been exciting for a long time. Even before she ended up in 1985 and became entangled with time travelling alien kidnappers and fake alien princes from the future, was eating cake under a tree a million years ago just a normal part of her life?

'Should we feed it some?' Fred asked.

Before she could answer, there was a rustle from a nearby patch of tall grass. She put a hand over Fred's mouth and pointed in the direction of the noise, holding her breath.

The grass moved and a long, slender figure stepped out, clutching a spear in its hand. Dressed in little more than rags around their waist and groin, it looked like one of the ancient aboriginals she had seen in the display in the museum.

Lucy didn't dare say a word as she watched the aboriginal, spear in hand, creep slowly towards the unsuspecting Diprotodon. Two more emerged from the grass behind them. She didn't know whether to feel relieved that the locals' attention hadn't fallen on them or worried for the poor Diprotodon, who was still pleasantly munching on his lunch of leaves.

Fred pulled her mouth away. 'Should we say something?' Fred whispered.

Lucy shook her head. 'We'd only startle them. I think the best thing we can do is get out of here before they realise that we are watching them.'

They stepped out of the shade of the tree directly into the sunlight, moving as quickly as they could towards a small outcrop of rocks. Lucy was worried that the aboriginals would spot them and turn their attention – and spears – in their direction.

When they reached the rocks, Lucy looked back. Fortunately, there was no sign of anyone pursuing them, but she didn't want to take any chances. Carefully, she climbed up onto the first ledge, gingerly grabbing the hot rock that had been baking in the sun. She had almost got used to the sweat and heat, but every so often, she grimaced as a boiling bit of stone touched her fingers.

They pulled themselves onto the ledge and saw the three aboriginals in the distance chasing the

Diprotodon. Despite how big it was, it was making some distance from its hunters. Lucy really hoped it got away.

'What now?' Fred said with a croak.

Her mouth was dry too and they had already run out of drink. 'You think there'd be a stream or pool in these rocks.'

Fred looked behind them, peering into the maze of rocks, with its crevices and sandy natural paths. There were small outcrops of grass everywhere, suggesting that there had to be water somewhere.

'Let's go find out.'

'And hopefully, we can get out of this sun,' Lucy said, licking her dry, cracked lips. She had never felt so hot. Her darker skin might protect her a little; poor Fred, even with his Australian blood, was as red as a tomato.

Carefully, they crawled over the ledge and slid down into a path between two huge natural columns of stone. They were immediately covered in shade, and it felt good to have the sun off their faces again. They paused just long enough to catch their breaths and began navigating their way through the rocks. All they needed was water and a cave.

They hadn't been walking long, when Lucy heard something, scrambling along the rocks above them. She looked up nervously.

'What is it?' Fred asked nervously.

'Might be my imagination. Let's keep going.'

They took another step, before Lucy heard a low, guttural growl. It reminded her of a cat, only much louder. She looked up again and gasped. A few feet away, was a large animal, the size of a lion or a tiger. Its jaw housed four long fangs and its eyes were fixed on them. Lucy didn't need Fred to look at the museum leaflet to tell her what it was.

A Thylacoleo Carnifex!

# CHAPTER TWELVE

# HUNTED

Fred was stuck somewhere in the middle between terrified and amazed. The real life Thylacoleo Carnifex was huge. A sort of lion with fangs that reminded him of the sabre tooth tigers he had seen in books, but with claws rather than paws at the end of its long feet. Its huge glassy eyes were focused right on him.

Terror quickly won out.

'Fred, we need to run!' Lucy said, grabbing his arm.

They ran down the narrow path between two large outcrops of rock. Luckily for them, the gap between the ledges above seemed too narrow for the Thylacoleo Carnifex to climb down and attack them.

But it was still terrifying to feel small rocks and stone clattering down the slope behind him and a fierce roar. As they ran, he could hear something scrambling over the rock nearby, but the one time he dared to look behind him, there was nothing.

'Is it there?' Lucy asked desperately, between panted breaths.

'No,' Fred replied. 'I think it's still up above us.'

Which meant the moment the path widened, it would jump down and kill them. Fred kept running, panting, and sweating in the suffocating heat. Even though the shadowy path was shielded from most of the sun, it was still baking hot, and his thin shirt was soaked to the skin.

A beam of light poured down through the rocks as the path opened up ahead. Fred held Lucy back, slowing their run to a jaunt as they neared the opening. There was no sight or sound of the Thylacoleo Carnifex, but that didn't mean it wasn't there. Slowly, carefully, they stepped out into the sunlight.

With a roar, the creature pounced, its claws clattering across loose rock as it leapt over a high ledge. Fred and Lucy both screamed as they broke into a run, desperately trying to reach another narrower path up ahead.

The Thylacoleo Carnifex landed with a thud on the ground, looking at them with those fierce eyes. As Fred stood frozen with fear, Lucy reached down and grabbed a sharp rock from the ground. With grim determination in her eyes, she threw the rock at the creature, hitting it in the face. It hesitated, letting out a low growl and took a couple of steps back.

Fred followed suit, grabbing another rock, and throwing it at the Thylacoleo Carnifex. The rock hit it in the shoulder. Lucy followed with a third, well-aimed rock to the face and this time it scuttled back to the edge of the wide opening, it's back legs gingerly stepping up onto the steep slope.

'Fred, let's go!' Lucy said, grabbing another rock and dragging him away.

Lucy flung her rock in the creature's direction. It missed this time, but it got the idea and held off its pursuit. They reached another narrow path and quickly scrambled to safety.

They could hear the Thylacoleo Carnifex again, but it was still too large to fit through the gap and they soon lost it. The path through the tall rocks was like a maze. Fred had no idea where they were going on and what they were going to do next.

Only when they were certain they were no longer being hunted, did they finally stop to rest.

Fred slumped against the smooth wall of rock. His heart was racing, and his mouth was as dry as the dirt and sand around them. He wished they hadn't finished the last of their spare drink.

Lucy wiped her brow, taking a few deep breaths. 'We need to find water,' she gasped.

Fred nodded. 'But where? There's nothing here

but rock, rock and more rock.'

'We saw trees and bushes, so there must be a water supply nearby,' she replied. 'I still say we need to find a cave or path under these rocks. There's sure to be water there.'

The sound of the Thylacoleo Carnifex roaring nearby filled the air and echoed through the narrow path. It sounded distant, though not far enough away for his liking.

'Okay, let's keep going before it finds us.'

'Agreed,' Lucy said. 'Oh, and I'm sorry.'

Fred frowned. 'Sorry for what?'

'I was thinking what it must be like to see a real Thylacoleo Carnifex. I didn't imagine the time ring would bring us here.'

'Do you think you can focus your mind on getting us out of here?'

Lucy shook her head. 'I've tried a few times. Come on, let's keep going.'

It seemed like they were walking forever. Fred's feet were hurting now. His Nike Dunks were not cut out for the Pleistocene period. Worst of all, his head was pounding from the heat. The shade did little to help with that.

'What's that?' Lucy asked, putting out a hand to stop him.

'What?' he asked, rubbing his temples.

'That? Can you hear it?'

Fred concentrated. It wasn't the Thylacoleo Carnifex. Was that… it sounded like trickling water.

'A stream?'

'Come on!' Lucy said with a grin. He followed her through the narrow path and sure enough, the sound of running water got louder.

Ahead of them was a larger opening, where a small running stream glistened in the sunlight. They ran towards it.

They were so hot and thirsty that the Thylacoleo Carnifex didn't cross either of their minds while they scooped up the cold water in their hands, took a drink, and then splashed some more on their faces.

'Fill the bottle,' Lucy suggested, and Fred quickly obliged, taking the empty pop bottle from his rucksack, and filling it. He handed it to her, and she guzzled the whole lot in one go. He refilled and did the same.

And then that familiar, dreaded growl came again. It was closer than last time. Fred hurriedly filled the bottle one more time and shoved it back in his rucksack.

'Look!' Lucy said, pointing at the water. See how it runs over there, behind that large boulder and into the rockface?'

'You think there might be a cave there?'

'We have to find somewhere to hide.'

Fred followed Lucy round the boulder, following

the path of the stream as it rolled down a small ledge and under a gap in the rock. It was just big enough to crawl through.

'What do you think?' Lucy asked nervously as they crept closer.

'It's worth a try,' Fred replied. 'Better than staying here and becoming that thing's dinner.'

They crouched down close to the water so that it almost touched their bellies as they crawled under the opening in the rock. The growl echoed through the air behind them, encouraging them to keep moving.

Fortunately, the opening was the lowest part of the tunnel. As they scrambled through, the roof began to rise, revealing a much larger cavern beyond. It was pitch black, but fortunately Fred had a torch in his rucksack. He liked to be prepared for all occasions. They soon had a wide beam of white light to guide the way as they followed the stream inside.

'Well, we got our cave,' Fred said, his voice echoing in the cool darkness. Between the water splashing over their feet and the lack of sun, this place was positively delightful.

'I suggest we wait here a while to get our strength back and then try and find a way back out of these rocks,' Lucy replied.

'Maybe try the time ring again?'

Lucy peered intently at the ring on her finger, but there was no glow. It obviously didn't work on command. Or at least, she didn't know how to command it.

Something small scurried out of the glow of torchlight on the wall ahead. Australia had its fair share of dangerous and poisonous creepy crawlies. He could only imagine what might be here in the Pleistocene period. Hopefully they would keep out of the light.

The stream ended abruptly, disappearing into the ground. 'What now?' he asked sitting down on a large boulder. He stuck the torch in the ground between them to give them some light.

Lucy sat down on a rock opposite him and sighed. 'I don't know. I've had enough of this place now.'

'Me too,' he agreed glumly. He was hot, tired, and hungry. And he had had quite enough of being hunted. He just wanted to go home. This must be what it felt like for Lucy. Only with more monsters.

Fred unzipped his rucksack and took out the bottle. He handed it to Lucy, who took a sip and then drank some himself. As he twisted the cap back on, something scratched near their feet. Fred looked down nervously and saw a small creature. It was not much bigger than a guinea pig or a rabbit and it looked a little like a cat. It sniffed the torch curiously.

'Is that…?' Lucy began anxiously.

As small as it was, it looked exactly like the big creature that had been hunting them outside. A baby Thylacoleo Carnifex.

Lucy looked at him, wide-eyed. 'Are we in its lair?'

Two more creatures appeared, shuffling around in the darkness. 'We need to get out of here!' Fred yelled.

A growl filled the cavern, filling him with dread. He grabbed his rucksack and lifted it over his shoulder, his hand trembling.

On the far side of the large cave was not one, but three Thylacoleo Carnifexes.

Lucy screamed as the creatures began to move slowly towards them. Their beady eyes were lit up in the torchlight, making them somehow more menacing.

'We won't make it.' He gasped, his heart pounding in his chest. Even if they could run to the cave opening, they wouldn't have time to crawl through to safety.

The first Thylacoleo Carnifex began moving quickly towards them, snarling.

'Fred!'

He spun around and saw the ring on Lucy's finger start to glow. He leapt towards her and grabbed her arm just in time. The last thing he saw was all three Thylacoleo Carnifexes running towards them as a flash of white light took them out of the cave...

# CHAPTER THIRTEEN

# A NATIONAL HERO

Lucy almost knocked a startled woman off her feet. The woman, dressed in a black dress and bonnet, gave her an angry look, and carried on walking, muttering something disparaging under her breath.

Where was she?

Lucy and Fred weren't in the Pleistocene period anymore. There were on a busy street, filled with people all dressed in their best finery. Men in top hats, women in dresses that covered them from their neck all the way to their feet. They all looked very old fashioned. She was certain she had read about people like this in books and seen them on TV.

'This isn't 1985,' Fred said, staring up and down the busy street.

'I think we should be glad we're not in that cave anymore,' Lucy said with a shudder, remembering the three Thylacoleo Carnifexes running in their direction. They had been a few seconds off becoming dinner.

'Agreed,' Fred replied. 'Come on, let's look around.'

Lucy followed him down the street, navigating their way through the crowd of people. They passed a couple of horse drawn carriages and the air smelt like something you would find in a sewer, but it was still preferable to where they had been.

Along the side of the street was a park. On the other side, Lucy could see the masts of several sailing ships. Whatever this place was, it was on the coast. Could it be Melbourne in another time?

Fred approached one man with a monocle over one eye and a huge twirling moustache on this face. 'Excuse me, kind sir. Could you kindly tell me where we are, kindly?'

The man gave a snort, glared at them both and muttered something about urchins as he carried on his way.

'Well, that was rude,' Fred scoffed. He turned to a woman with a hat almost as wide as she was tall.

'Good day to you, madam.'

The woman looked a little startled and gave Lucy a disparaging frown.

'Good day, to you,' the woman replied cautiously. 'What can I do for you and your…*friend*?'

Lucy didn't like the tone in the woman's voice,

but she ignored it. They needed answers.

'I was kindly wondering if you would kindly tell me where we are, kindly.'

'Ashworth Street.'

'Yes, but what town or city, kindly, please? Kindly?'

Lucy wasn't convinced he had this whole old-fashioned speaking down, but the woman at least, seemed a little bemused.

'Why, Melbourne of course.'

'Oh, that's a relief, I think. Kindly. And kindly, what year is this, kindly, please?'

'What an odd question,' the woman replied. Her smile dropped and there was suspicion in her look. 'Who are you? Why are you here and why are you dressed like that? With this, *aboriginal* girl?'

'We're, er...'

'We were supposed to be working on the docks,' Lucy said quickly. She didn't like the fact that the woman called her aboriginal, just because of the colour of her skin. But now was not the time to argue.

'Hmmm...' the woman turned her gaze back to Fred. 'Why do you want to know the year?' She paused, 'Ah, I guess a lack of education leads to a lack of knowledge. I would expect it from her kind.'

*Her kind*?

Lucy was about to explode, but Fred stepped beside her, laying a reassuring hand on her shoulder.

'Please, madam. Could you kindly tell us the year? Kindly please?'

'Why it's 1895, of course,' she said and quickly shuffled away in her big dress and hat.

'I didn't like her.' Lucy scowled as she watched the woman continue down the street. 'Looking down on people like that.'

'I know, I'm sorry,' Fred said with a reassuring smile. 'At least we know where and *when* we are.'

'There is that.' She sighed. 'Come one, let's find somewhere a little quieter. I don't like the way people are looking at us.'

They headed towards the park, where a large crowd was gathering near a pavilion. Most of them were women, all dressed in the same variation of big hats, dresses and carrying parasols.

'What's going on?' Fred asked as they approached the back of the crowd.

Lucy shrugged. She could see a woman on the pavilion stand. She was older, maybe sixty or seventy, wearing a tightly buttoned black dress adorned with white lace around her neck and sleeves. There was more lace in her hair, that had been tightened into a bun at the back. She looked terribly important.

'We have fought long and hard for this victory and I am grateful to every one of you for your support. As vice president of the Women's Suffrage

League, I am proud of the passion, determination and struggles we have faced to get to this point! We are women, and we will be heard!'

'Who is she?' Lucy asked curiously, trying to get a better view between two women with extremely large hats.

One of the women heard and turned her in excitement. 'Do you not know? That is the great Catherine Helen Spence!'

The woman turned back, eager to hear every word from the woman on the stage. Lucy looked at Fred questioningly. 'Well, people seem to like her. Do you know anything about her?'

Fred grinned. 'History buff, remember? We discussed her in school last year. She led the Women's Equal Franchise Association here in Australia. She was largely responsible for women getting the right to vote.'

'Wow,' Lucy gasped, a sense of pride swelling within her. This woman was a hero.

Catherine Helen Spence continued her speech. 'I have spoken at events in Britain and the USA. I have campaigned on your behalf for women's suffrage and electoral reform. It was an honour to speak at the Chicago World's Fair in 1893.

'But for me, coming home to Australia and knowing that South Australia has become the first Australian colony, and the fourth place in the world, to grant women's suffrage, is what brings me the greatest joy!'

There was a huge round of applause from the crowd and Lucy joined in wholeheartedly. It was because of women like this Catherine Helen Spence that she would have the rights, many would take for granted, when she became an adult.

She didn't know why they had come here, whether it was on purpose, or by accident. But she felt a deep honour to hear this woman speaking.

'Not only that,' Catherine added, raising her finger importantly. 'But we have also been granted, for the first time, the right to stand for election to Parliament, the first place in the world to do so. It is a privilege and a right that I shall embrace with all my heart!'

The crowd erupted in applause once again and once again, Lucy joined in. Fred clapped too. She was glad she could share this special moment with him.

As the crowed grew silent, Catherine spoke again. 'I am a new woman, and I know it. I mean I am an awakened woman, awakened into a sense of capacity and responsibility, not merely to the family and household, but to the state: to be wise, not for her own selfish interests, but that the world may be glad that she had been born.'

Lucy beamed from ear to ear. But beside her, Fred

shuffled awkwardly.

'What's wrong she asked quietly?'

'I don't know,' Fred replied. 'I thought I felt something digging into my back.'

'What have you got in there?'

'Just the usual supplies…' Fred began, taking the rucksack off his shoulders.

Something was moving inside. 'Come on, let's find somewhere quieter to investigate,' she told him and led him away from the crowd. It looked as if Catherine's speech was almost done.

They found a large tree close to the edge of Ashworth Street and settled down under the branches. Fred laid the backpack on the ground and unzipped it.

Lucy jumped out of her skin as something crawled out of the rucksack. It was small, with a long tail and tiny little claws.

A baby Thylacoleo Carnifex!

'How did that get in there!' Lucy gasped.

Fred stared at her, his eyes wide in disbelief. 'It must have crawled inside when I took out the water in the cave!'

'Well, quick, put it back inside!'

Fred gingerly moved his hands to lure the baby Thylacoleo Carnifex inside the backpack. It let out a small yelp and he jumped back.

'I, I can't!' he stammered.

'Let me do it!' she said with determination, trying to shove it back inside. She almost had the open rucksack over the creature when it leaped over her wrist and bounded across the grass.

Fred grabbed the rucksack and he and Lucy began running towards the grass as it made several big leaps with astonishing speed. Before they could stop the Thylacoleo Carnifex, it was on the street.

It was too fast to catch. Lucy and Fred ran into the street heading towards the sea. If it got on one of those ships, they had no chance stopping it!

Lucy froze in horror, starring at the baby Thylacoleo Carnifex as it disappeared out of sight. There was a deadly, ancient creature loose in nineteenth century Melbourne and it was all their fault!

# CHAPTER FOURTEEN

# DANGER AT THE DOCKS

Fred had never felt so guilty in all his life. If he hadn't opened his backpack in that cave, the baby Thylacoleo Carnifex would never have crawled inside, and he would never have brought it here to 1895.

What if it killed everyone? What if it ate his grandmother's grandmother? Would Melbourne still be as he remembered it back in 1985? His parent's video store? Space/Time Books? Would it all be there when they eventually got back?

If they got back.

As they searched down another alley, Fred realised that his excitement about travelling through time had vanished. Now he was tired and scared and afraid he would never get back home again.

'What now?' asked Lucy with exasperation.

She looked just as exhausted as him. At least her

dark skin had fared better than his in the Pleistocene Period. The skin on his arms was red and raw and his face felt sore under the brim of his cap.

'I need to rest,' he groaned, slumping to the ground, and resting his back against a brick wall.

The alley wasn't exactly clean, but he was past caring. There was a stink about the place that had caused him to gag more than once. Nineteenth century Melbourne was a bit stinky.

'Let's head to the docks,' Lucy suggested. 'There's a chance we might spot it out in the open.'

'Or we just follow the screams?' he said drolly.

Lucy gave him a stern look. 'There's no use sulking. We *have* to find it.'

Fred nodded reluctantly. With a groan, he pulled himself up. 'Okay, let's keep searching.'

The sea breeze blowing in over the coast was a mix of fresh salty air and something you would get in an unflushed toilet. It all depended which way the wind was blowing on which smell you got.

They wandered the docks aimlessly. There were several large ships, and crates and boxes everywhere with workmen moving back and forth. It was hard to find any sign of the baby Thylacoleo Carnifex.

Rather surprisingly, they didn't get any dirty looks down here, particularly Lucy. It seemed that these men didn't really care about two unkempt youths wearing t-shirts, shorts, and baseball caps.

Not that what they were wearing was suitable nineteenth century attire. Fred took a mental note; next time you are time travelling, take a period-appropriate wardrobe with you.

'There it is!' Lucy cried, pointing towards a wooden walkway between two ships.

Fred saw the baby Thylacoleo Carnifex, crawling between two crates, making no sound. It seemed as if the workmen on the docks hadn't noticed it.

They ran after the baby Thylacoleo Carnifex, but it was quicker than they were. It scrambled up one very large wooden box and leapt to another and then another. It was moving very quickly, away from the ships, but they were far too slow, and too low, to catch it.

Lucy grabbed Fred's hand and led him down a long, narrow path between the crates. They found the baby Thylacoleo Carnifex trying to reach the edge of one box, looking for a way down.

'What we really need is a net.' Fred sighed.

'I wished we had grabbed one over by the ships. I saw a few tied up.'

'Well, it's no use going back now,' he groaned. 'We'll never find it if we go back. It looks like it's about to jump. We could try and catch it?'

'With those claws?' Lucy shook her head. 'It would scratch us to pieces.'

Fred had to admit she was right. It was only a

baby, but it still had sharp claws and fangs. 'I've got an idea,' he said, lifting the backpack off his shoulders. 'If I whack it when it jumps down, maybe I can stun it long enough to put it back in the backpack.'

'Don't kill it!' Lucy said with alarm, and then added, 'Be careful!'

The baby Thylacoleo Carnifex made a giant leap off the huge wooden box onto the ground. Fred swung the backpack furiously, but it barely grazed the creature. It hit the ground, pausing momentarily, but not long enough for Fred to tear open the backpack.

Lucy desperately reached for it, seemingly forgetting everything she had said about the claws, but it nimbly leapt over her arm and began running across the open space towards the crates at the other side.

Before they could even catch a breath, it disappeared.

'What do we do now?' Fred gasped, his heart racing.

Lucy put her hands on her waist and leaned over, catching her breath. 'We follow and try again.'

They took a moment to drink from the bottle of spring water from the Pleistocene Period and then continued their search. But as they entered the next part of the docks, they heard something new. Gun shots.

Fred froze. 'Do you think someone found the baby Thylacoleo Carnifex?' he asked nervously.

Lucy looked just as worried. 'Maybe. Let's keep moving but be *really* quiet.'

They soon found themselves near another ship, tethered away from the rest. The walkway seemed deserted and at first there was no sign of the baby Thylacoleo Carnifex or whoever had fired that gun.

'Stay back!'

Two men charged onto the walkway. They both wore black coats, white shirts, and cravats. One of them was wearing a bowler hat and the other had an impressive moustache that twirled at the end. Both had guns in their hands.

Fred took a step back nervously, clutching Lucy's trembling hand, but the men blocked their escape. They were trapped!

The man with the moustache put his gun in his holster. The man in the bowler hat kept his, though his attention was on the walkway, rather than them.

'Good God!' the moustached man gasped. 'What in all King's good country are you both doing here?'

'I, I'm…' Fred fumbled for words.

'We're looking for our pet cat,' Lucy jumped in quickly. 'Have you seen it?'

Well, that was sort of the truth.

The man looked at them in disbelief. 'Your cat?

No, I don't know that I have. But this place is dangerous! You shouldn't be here.'

'Cedric!' the other man exclaimed sharply. 'We need to keep going. The Gilded Serpent Society are still out here.'

'What's the Gilded Serpent Society?' Fred asked curiously.

'None of your business,' the moustached man, Cedric, replied with a sharp glare, turning to the other man. 'And may I remind you, *Cecil*, that we should keep our activities to ourselves?'

'They're just children,' Cecil scoffed. 'Come on, we need to find them before they board the ship.'

Cedric looked back at Fred and Lucy suspiciously. 'I would advise you to find somewhere safe that is not here. There are dangerous criminals afoot, and I would be mortified if you were caught in the crossfire.'

'Criminals?' Fred asked, half with alarm, half with excitement. 'Is that what the Gilded Serpent Society are?'

'Do you *understand* me, boy?'

Fred nodded sheepishly. 'I understand.'

Cedric turned to Lucy with the same, heavy stare. 'And you, young madam?'

'My name's Lucy, and yes, I understand,' she replied curtly.

'Good, stay safe,' Cedric said with a nod, taking

out his gun and joining Cecil.

The two strange men walked off. Fred looked at Lucy. 'What do you think that was all about?'

Lucy shrugged. 'Well, if it's to do with criminals, I think it's best we did as we were told and found somewhere safe.'

'It can't be any more dangerous than the Thylacoleo Carnifex lair.'

'Yes, but if they have guns, I assume this Gilded Serpent Society will have guns too. And guns can be just as dangerous.'

'I guess,' Fred said, his mind still racing. The Gilded Serpent Society? It sounded magical and exciting. Like something from a pirate story or a James Bond film.

Something ran across the walkway behind the two men. It was quick, but it was unmistakable. The baby Thylacoleo Carnifex.

It ran behind a wooden shack. Fred took a deep breath, grabbed Lucy's hand and together they darted across the walkway before Cedric and Cecil could spot them. By the time they reached the shack, the creature was gone.

They were careful to stay out of sight as they continued their search near the sailing ship. Fred was worried that it might get onboard.

Suddenly, they heard the shouting and several crates fell to the ground. Crouched behind one crate, they watched as Cedric and Cecil stepped back on the walkway near them, searching for something, or someone. Fred presumed they were fighting with this Gilded Serpent Society. He kept hidden with Lucy. Now was not the time to try and run.

A third man appeared further up the walkway, dressed like Cedric and Cecil in a long grey coat. He holstered his gun as he approached the others. One of the men, Cedric, continued to search their surroundings, while Cecil and the new man talked.

'What do you think is going on?' Fred whispered to Lucy.

She looked at him and shrugged. 'They look worried, whatever it is.'

'Who do you think they are?' Fred pondered. 'The police? Spies?'

'I just hope they are the good guys,' Lucy said glumly.

'Well, they didn't hurt us, so I guess they must be.'

Fred liked action and adventure, but the reality of seeing men fighting each other was far less exciting and far more likely to get them killed. They were better staying hidden where it was safe.

Cedric and Cecil ran off, leaving the third man on his own. Suddenly there was another man, dressed similarly to the others, with a gun in his hand, climbing across the crates and boxes very close to Fred and Lucy.

He looked a little fiercer; maybe that was the scar running down his cheek, but he looked distinctly… bad.

The man that had been talking with Cedric and Cecil was completely unaware, as he walked right past them. The man with the scar crept to the edge of the crate just a couple of feet from where they were hiding and aimed his gun. Fred realised that the man was going to be killed, but it was Lucy who acted.

'Watch out!' she cried, leaping, and bravely pushing the crate out from under the man's feet. The man with the scar gave a cry, dropping his gun and crashing to the ground with a thud. Cedric and Cecil's friend was on his attacker in an instant, tying his hands behind his back to stop him escaping.

Cedric and Cecil returned as the third man turned his attention to Fred and Lucy.

'You saved my life,' the third man said.

'Er, thanks?' Lucy replied awkwardly.

'I thought I told you both to stay away?' Cedric said crossly.

The third man smiled, as he passed the bound criminal to Cedric. 'Well, I am glad that they didn't.' He looked back to Lucy. 'On behalf of the three of us, you have my thanks.'

Fred stepped out, taking them all by surprise. 'Is

he one of the Gilded Serpent Society?' he asked hesitantly.

The third man looked at Cedric questioningly. 'How do they know about them, Cedric?'

'I believe it was Cecil,' Cedric said sheepishly

'My apologies, Alistair,' Cecil said.

The third man, Alistair, shook his head. 'I would expect officers of British Intelligence to be trained in the art of discretion.'

'British Intelligence?' Fred gasped.

Cedric laughed. 'We did not mention who we were, Alistair.'

'Well then,' Alistair sighed. 'Perhaps it is time to bring this conversation to a close. Come, we have a ship to board. Europe awaits us.'

'What's in Europe?' Lucy asked.

'None of your business, young girl,' Alistair said. 'But know you have my gratitude.' He smiled. 'Alistair Lethbridge-Stewart at your service.'

Lucy froze. Fred thought there was recognition on her face. The three men bowed their heads and marched their captive onto the ship, leaving them on the walkway.

'What is it?' Fred asked.

'That name...' Lucy frowned. 'I recognise that name. I think it was my grandfather's.'

Fred did the calculation in his head. 'Your grandfather. But that doesn't make any sense. You're from the early twenty-first century, right?'

'Right?'

'Well, if he was your grandfather, that would make him well over a hundred years old.'

Lucy nodded. 'I guess you're right. Maybe it's a distant relative then.'

'I guess,' Fred shrugged. 'Okay, shall we keep searching for the baby Thylacoleo Carnifex?'

'I guess so…' Lucy froze. 'Fred!'

The ring on Lucy's finger began to glow. Fred instinctively grabbed her hand, just in time for the white light to carry them away…

# CHAPTER FIFTEEN

# THE FIRST FLEET

Fred felt a blast of sea breeze on his face the moment the white light faded. It wasn't the rank, sewage stink of the Melbourne docks. It was clean, refreshing and cooled his face.

It took him a moment to realise that they were standing on top of a cliff, looking out over the sea. There were no buildings around them, just grass, sand, rocks, and trees. But out on the water, he could make out several ships, with tall masts and flags like something out of a pirate movie.

'Where are we?' Lucy asked nervously.

Fred shrugged. 'I don't know. I'm guessing we haven't gone back to the Pleistocene era, by the look of those ships.'

'The baby Thylacoleo Carnifex!' she said with a gasp. 'We didn't catch it!'

'It must still be in 1895,' Fred said, feeling guilt swell up in his stomach. 'We lost it. It's all my fault.'

'No, it's not,' she said, putting a hand reassuringly on his shoulder. 'We did our best.'

He wasn't convinced. 'Do you think it ate anyone? What if it killed someone important? What if it ate Catherine Helen Spence or that Alistair Lethbridge-Stewart? What if history was changed?'

Lucy sighed. 'Well, we can't do anything about it now.' But it got her back to thinking about her family tree.

Fred sighed again and looked out to the sea. The breeze was quite pleasant, and the sun was warm, but not too hot. He'd had enough of baking to death in the heat. He would do anything for a swimming pool or good air conditioning.

'Let's get a closer look,' he said, and lead her down a narrow, rocky path closer to the beach.

The lead ship was moving slowly towards the coast. As they reached a natural plateau in the side of the cliff, half was down, Fred spotted movement on the beach below.

'Look,' he said with a gasp, pointing to the group of people gathering to watch the vessel. They were clearly aboriginal, with dark skin that was like hers. They seemed to be carrying what looked like fishing rods and spears. One of them was carrying a canoe on his back.

'Who do you think they are?' Lucy asked.

'I don't know,' he said, frowning as he looked at

the lead ship. It had two tall masts and flags at the front and back. They carried the Union Jack. A British vessel. Were these settlers? Had they gone back through time, rather than forward?

'I think I can make out a name of the ship,' Fred said, creasing his eyes and shielding them from the sun with his hand. 'The… HMS Supply!'

He looked at her excitedly, but she wasn't paying the ship, or him, any real attention.

'Oh, I think my grandfather's grandfather had the same name,' Lucy said just as excitedly. 'Could that have been him? Did I just save my *great, great* grandfather's life?'

That sounded like an awfully big coincidence, but this was far more exciting. 'Lucy, it's the HMS Supply! Botany Bay!'

Lucy frowned. 'I think I remember something about Botany Bay. Wasn't that the first British ship to arrive in Australia?'

Fred nodded. 'Well, you're half right. The first British ship to arrive in Australia was the HMS Endeavour under the command of Captain Cook. I'm trying to remember the date. Was it 1770?'

He looked at Lucy questioningly, but she just shrugged.

'I don't know,' Lucy said. 'I just remember the name Botany Bay. But you said that's the HMS Supply?'

'Yes, that arrived later with the First Fleet, under the command of Captain Phillip. He brought the first people to settle in Australia and the HMS Supply was his ship.'

Lucy frowned. 'They're settlers?'

'Convicts mostly,' Fred replied. 'It's probably best if we stay out of sight when they arrive.'

Lucy pointed nervously to the group of Aboriginal people gathered on the beach. 'What about them. What happens to the locals?'

Fred looked at her glumly. 'It's not good. The settlers completely displace them, enslave them. I think a lot of them die of cholera.'

'Oh, that's awful!' Lucy said.

'They're called…' Fred frowned in concentration. He did know this! 'I think they're called the Eora.'

'I thought they were aboriginals?'

'They are. The Eora is what the settlers name them.'

'Then I shall call them aborigines,' Lucy said defiantly.

They watched as the HMS Supply sailed closer. It seemed exciting and fascinating and frightening and oppressive at the same time.

Despite the danger and all the horrible things these settlers would do to the locals, Fred couldn't help but feel a surge of excitement. He was watching history unfold. Everything he had read in books was coming to life before his very eyes!

Lucy was looking at the time ring on her finger. 'Why did it bring us here?'

Fred frowned. As exciting and as scary as this all was, each trip through time seemed rather random. 'I don't know. The Pleistocene period kind of made sense. We were thinking about the Thylacoleo Carnifex.'

'And maybe I jumbled up the numbers in my head when we went to 1895,' Lucy suggested. 'Maybe I crossed the nine and the eight. I thought 1895 instead of 1985.'

'Perhaps,' Fred said half-heartedly. He was still feeling guilty about losing the baby Thylacoleo Carnifex.

'That still doesn't explain why we came here.' Lucy said with a frown. 'What year is this?'

'It was eighteen years between Captain Cook's arrival and Captain Phillips. So, 1788?'

'Well then, hopefully we'll go forward in time next time?'

'Unless we go back. What if we end up back at the Big Bang?'

'Then I don't think we're coming back from that,' Lucy shuddered. 'Okay, 1788. Is there a reason for this time? Or is the time ring just acting randomly?'

'I wish I knew.'

*

They found a small cave at the bottom of the cliffs, away from the water, where they could watch the arrival of the First Fleet. When the HMS Supply got closer, the aborigines fled. At least they had sense to hide from the strangers to their land.

Fred and Lucy finished off the last remnants of fruit cake from the backpack, keenly aware that they had no idea where their next meal was going to come from. He had lost track of how long it had been since the museum in Melbourne. It might have been hours. It might have been days. He felt exhausted, but not quite 'staying awake for three days exhausted', so maybe the trips through time had been shorter than he realised.

Hoping that the men on the First Fleet wouldn't find them, they decided to catch a few hours' sleep. Fred's last memory was of the brilliant reds and purples of the setting sun rippling over the calm waters, before tiredness overcome him and he laid his head on his backpack.

When Fred awoke, it was completely dark. It took him a moment to remember where he was. For a terrifying second, he thought he was back in the cave with the Thylacoleo Carnifexes trying to eat him.

There was a ripple of moonlight at the edge of the small cave, and he sat there, panting for breath, watching Lucy, who was still sound asleep, her head on her rolled-up hoody. The only sound, besides his frightened breaths, came from the ocean. The waves lashing against the rocks nearby was rather soothing.

He was just about to wake Lucy up when he heard a scream.

Lucy jumped up, her eyes bright and awake. 'What was that?'

'I, I don't know,' Fred replied nervously. 'Come on, let's find out.'

Lucy picked up her hoody and tied it around her waist as Fred pulled the straps of his backpack over his shoulders. They stepped outside the cave, afraid that the men of the First Fleet might be lying in wait for them.

Thankfully there was no sign of anyone at the cave entrance. There were several fires burning on the beach below, where the men of the First Fleet had obviously set up camp. Fred and Lucy both agreed that they needed to avoid that place as much as possible.

The scream rang out over the night air again, a panicked, terrified scream. It wasn't coming from the camp, but the grassy slope above.

'Come on!' he said, grabbing Lucy's wrist and leading her through the rocks and grassy outcrops that ran along the path away from the cave. He was grateful that there was enough moonlight to guide them, so they didn't trip and fall. The path ran along the cliff's edge and he didn't feel like taking a swim.

He soon saw a group of figures silhouetted in the moonlight. Fred and Lucy crouched low, careful to remain hidden. There were three men, Caucasian men, with white shirts and dark trousers, who seemed to be closing in on a group of aboriginals. They looked like a family. A man, a woman and two children.

'We've got to help them,' Lucy muttered fiercely.

'How?' Fred asked desperately. 'We don't have any weapons and I don't fancy going up against them with nothing but my bare hands.'

One of the men laughed and reached for the woman. The mum? The man, the dad, stepped in front her and the children, and shouted something aggressively. The three men in the white shirts stepped back, obviously taken aback by the tone of his voice. Fred hoped he was able to defend his family.

There seemed to be an argument happening, but both groups were talking in different languages. One of the children, a girl, not much younger than him, screamed in terror and made a run for it.

Fred didn't know what to do. The three Caucasian men stepped back, but the little girl was already running down the grassy slope, looking for safety.

Unfortunately, she was heading straight for the camp.

Lucy looked at Fred. 'We've got to help out! Before the rest of the settlers find her!'

– CHAPTER SIXTEEN –
# SAVING DARANA

Lucy looked out over the beach, lit up by campfires, and felt a sense of dread. There were bits of knowledge floating around her brain that she remembered perfectly, glimpses of her own life. A school project, looking at the treatment of slaves, thrown onto ships from Africa in chains and forced to work for people in America, Europe, and the rest of the "civilised" world.

Well, there was nothing civil about it. If Fred was right, she had already witnessed the same thing happening here in Australia. These settlers had been here just a few hours and already they were destroying the lives of the people who lived here first.

She knew Fred wouldn't quite get what she was feeling. He was kind and compassionate and open-minded. But he wouldn't experience discrimination just for the colour of his skin. Not like she would.

Like she had, back in 1895. And, she had the uneasy feeling, even in her own time.

So, watching that aboriginal girl, with her dark skin, running towards the danger of these white settlers, she knew she had to save her.

Even if she could save one family, that might be enough. That might be the reason she was here, if there was reason to be found in any of this.

There had to be. If she had really saved her great, great grandfather's life, maybe there was a strange purpose to all of these trips through time.

They ran after the girl. The rest of the girl's family were somewhere behind them, and Lucy hoped the dad was able to stop the three men from hurting them.

'She's almost at the camp,' Fred said as they kept running. 'Doesn't she realise where she's going?'

'She's terrified,' Lucy replied, wiping sweat from her brow. 'When you're in a panic like that, your brain doesn't work. She's running to get away from those men. She doesn't know where, but she knows she needs to run.'

They lost the girl at the edge of the camp. Lucy and Fred slowed down and quietly crept past the nearest tent, making sure they stayed out of the light of the burning torches planted into the sand. They could hear the low rumbling of men talking nearby: laughter, arguing and singing. There was a stink of body odour and beer in the air.

It didn't feel like a safe place at all.

'Where is she?' Fred whispered as they slunk past the entrance of a tent. It was like a maze, and they could be spotted at any moment.

'She ran past here,' Lucy said, pointing at the sand before them. There were small footprints, lit up by the glow of the moon above them. They were too small to be an adult's. 'Let's follow them.'

Suddenly, they heard a yelp up ahead and they rushed towards the noise as quietly as they could manage. They found the girl near a campfire, trembling and crying, and she wasn't alone. There was a man with her, a huge man with a big bushy beard and a bald forehead dripping with sweat. His big, black eyes, lit up by the glow of the nearby campfire, were terrifying. He had a wicked smile on his face.

'What's we 'ave 'ere?' he cackled, as he moved towards the girl.

The girl mumbled something in her native language, and the man laughed.

'Wot, you don't speak the King's language, little girl? We'll soon 'ave you all civilised!'

He reached out and grabbed the girl's arm and she screamed. Lucy was terrified that that scream would attract the attention of the rest of the camp. She had to act now if they had any chance of saving the girl.

Fred looked at her questioningly and she pointed at the wooden torch in the ground. He picked it up carefully and she took it. Fred grabbed a large rock from the ground, and they nodded at each other.

They had to be brave.

Holding her breath, Lucy ran towards the large man. 'Let go of her!' she said fiercely, but not so loudly that it might attract the attention of anyone else.

Still holding the weeping girl by the arm, the man turned and looked at her with a wicked smile.

'Ah, more black brats!' he said with an almost toothless grin.

Lucy was having none of that. She flung the torch towards his face, the flames touching his beard and setting it alight. It wasn't enough to properly hurt him, and he quickly brushed the burning embers free. But he let go of the girl and that was enough for Lucy to reach out and grab her, dragging her behind her for protection.

'Oi, you little...'

He didn't get a chance to finish what he was saying. Fred flung the rock at the man, hitting him in the head and he stumbled backwards, falling into the nearest tent, and getting caught up in the ropes holding it together.

'Run!' Fred cried.

Lucy didn't need to be told twice. Still holding the girl's hand, they raced towards the edge of the camp. They heard a few cries behind them, but luckily there was no one to block their path. It took them less than a minute to reach the grassy slope at the edge of the beach and they didn't stop there.

Lucy wasn't sure she would ever stop running.

But eventually, the girl let go and Lucy felt the momentum push her forward into the grass. Lucy and the girl landed with a thump and for a moment she just lay there, gasping for breath, her head spinning and her heart thumping.

Fred reached out with a hand to pull her up. Her legs felt like jelly as she stumbled to her feet. The little girl was still sat on the ground, her cheeks wet with tears and sweat. Her eyes were huge, and she looked terrified.

Lucy took a step slowly towards her. 'You're safe,' she said, forcing a smile. 'The bad man is gone.'

'What about the other three?' Fred asked nervously.

Lucy hoped they wouldn't walk into them on the slope ahead. 'Hopefully they returned to the camp and left that family alone. We need to get her back to her parents.'

'If they're still okay.'

Lucy chose not to answer that. She looked at the girl and gave her another reassuring smile. 'Safe.

You're safe.'

The girl wiped away her tears and looked at Lucy with a quizzical expression. No doubt she was confused that Lucy's skin was a similar colour to hers, even though she wore clothing that probably resembled the people from the ships.

'I'm Lucy,' she said, tapping her chest. 'Lucy.' With another smile, she held out her hand and pointed at the girl's chest.

The girl frowned. Lucy tapped her own chest. 'Lucy.' She pointed to the girl again, hoping she would get the idea.

'Darana,' the girl replied cautiously.

Lucy smiled. 'Hello, Darana. Nice to meet you.' She turned to Fred. 'Your turn.'

Fred grinned and tapped his chest. 'Fred. Hello, Darana.'

Darana, if that was her name, eyed Fred more suspiciously. But then, he did look like the men that had attacked her and her family. She let out a little scowl.

Fred looked at Lucy awkwardly. 'Is this what it's like, when someone doesn't like you because of the colour of your skin?'

Lucy considered his question. The girl, Darana, had reason not to trust anyone who didn't look like her. 'Sort of,' she said.

'I'm sorry you went through that, with the

woman back in 1895.'

Lucy forced a smile because she knew that was what he needed to see. 'Thank you.'

There were sounds behind them, several voices at the edge of the camp. Darana gave a yelp of terror.

'Come on,' Fred said nervously. 'We're not far enough away.'

Lucy nodded and took Darana's hand. 'You're safe,' she said, smiling.

The three of them hurried up the slope, away from the beach, searching for Darana's family. The noise on the beach aside, the whole area felt oddly silent. Lucy assumed her family would be looking for her and really hoped they hadn't ventured down into the camp.

'*Duruninang!*'

A woman's cry echoed out across the night sky and Darana gave a yelp of joy.

'*Wiyanga!*'

What does that mean?' Fred asked.

Lucy shook her head. 'I don't know. Mother maybe?' She looked at Darana and pointed in the direction of the woman's cry. '*Wiyanga?*'

Lucy wasn't sure she had pronounced the word correctly, or if it was what she thought it meant, but Darana's nodded furiously.

The woman cried out again, her words muffled by a gust of wind, but loud enough that they could follow it.

'*Wiyanga*,' Darana said firmly and let go of Lucy's hand, breaking into a run. Lucy and Fred followed at a distance and soon enough, three figures appeared at the top of the hill. It was her parents and brother.

Darana ran into the woman's eyes and there were cries of elation from all four of them. Lucy watched, her heart swelling.

'Mob,' Fred muttered.

Lucy looked at him and frowned. '*Mob*?'

'It's the aboriginal word for family. I think. If school got it right, that is.'

'Thank you for helping me save Darana.'

Fred grinned back. 'I'm glad she's safe.'

'For now,' Lucy said with a sigh, watching as the father figure urged them away. Darana looked back briefly and then left, with her family. Her *mob*.

'Goodbye, Darana.'

There were more shouts coming from the camp. The three men that had accosted Darana's family walked over a nearby rocky ledge and caught sight of Lucy and Fred. She realised they were standing right in a pool of moonlight, clear for all to see.

'We've got to go!' Fred cried.

Lucy was about to agree, when she felt a warm flash on her hand as the time ring activated. 'Fred, grab my hand.'

He didn't need to be told twice. He took her hand, leaving Botany Bay behind them.

# CHAPTER SEVENTEEN

# AN UNEASY FUTURE

For a moment, Fred wondered if they were home. They had reappeared in the middle of a busy street, much to the surprise of a couple of passers-by. People were dressed in suits, t-shirts and shorts, dresses, jeans, and skirts. The sort of everyday clothing he was used to in Melbourne.

'Do you recognise this place?' Lucy asked curiously.

Fred shook his head. 'Melbourne's a big place, Lucy. I haven't been to every street.'

Lucy laughed. 'I'm sorry, I just meant, does this look like Melbourne?'

'I don't know. Maybe.'

He felt exhausted. The nap in the cave had helped, but he longed for his comfortable bed and one of his mum's home-cooked meals.

'I suggest we look around, get our bearings,' Lucy said. 'You got any money left?'

'Sure, but won't it be out-of-date?'

'Don't know, depends what year it is. Hang on, what's that?'

Something across the road was fluttering. Lucy dashed in-between the cars, almost causing a man on a bicycle to crash headfirst into a van. 'Sorry!' she shouted, as she raced along the pavement. With a theatrical dive, she grabbed the fluttering thing and held it up in the air.

'Twenty dollars,' she shouted.

'How lucky is that? Maybe we can get a drink and a sandwich,' said Fred, catching her up. 'Hang on, let me see.' Fred snatched the twenty dollars from Lucy's hand.

'Rude,' Lucy said.

'Look, it's made of plastic,' Fred said, holding it up to the light. 'We're definitely in the future.'

'I hope twenty is enough,' Lucy said. 'There's a sandwich shop over there. Shall we find out?'

Fred grinned. 'Sounds like a great idea.'

The sandwich shop was called Subway. Fred had never heard of the place, but they had plenty to choose from and soon they were munching on large rolls filled with salad, meat and cheese and consuming large cups of Coca-Cola. It felt almost as good to sit on a chair, as it was to have something nice to eat.

'I think the first thing we need to do is find out

the date,' Lucy suggested, between bites of her sandwich.

Fred nodded and took a slurp of his coke. 'Yeah, should be easier to ask someone this time.'

'Or we just find a newspaper?' Lucy suggested. 'No point sounding like crazies when we can find out for ourselves. We might even be able to find out if we're in Melbourne too.'

It was a solid plan. They finished up their meal and went in search of somewhere they could find a newspaper. After wandering for a couple of streets, they found a stand. Fred quickly rushed over to the stack of newspapers and scanned the front page.

*The Sun Herald*. He thought Melbourne might have that paper, but then he saw the by-line.

**All your local news from Sydney.**

He showed it to Lucy. 'At least we're still in Australia.'

'P Sherman, 42 Wallaby Way, Sydney,' Lucy blurted

'Pardon?' Fred asked, eyebrows raised.

'Nemo! It's from the film *Finding Nemo*. I just remembered it!' Lucy exclaimed. She had watched the film on repeat when she was little. She didn't know why she could remember that when she couldn't even remember her own family. Lucy shook her head. 'We're in the future too,' Lucy said, focusing her attention on the newspaper. '14th September 2000.'

'Wow,' Fred said. 'We've gone forward fifteen years this time.'

'At least we're closer than we were,' Lucy replied.

Fred grinned. The future? This was exciting. He wondered what had changed in the world since 1985.

Lucy was reading the newspaper intently, much to the chagrin of the man running the newspaper stand. 'Are you going to buy that?' he asked crossly. 'This isn't a library.'

'Oh, sorry,' Fred said sheepishly, handing the man some change for the paper. It was much more expensive than he was used to.

They walked away from the stand, Lucy still holding the paper as she read the article on the front page. She was so engrossed, she nearly walked into three pedestrians and a streetlamp.

'What's so interesting?' he asked curiously.

Lucy handed him the paper. 'Take a look at that.'

He read the headline. 'Local authorities staying quiet on recent bear attacks ahead of the Olympics opening ceremony.' He looked at Lucy hesitantly. 'Bear attacks?'

'You don't think it's the baby Thylacoleo Carnifex we lost in 1895?'

Lucy shook her head. 'I can't see how. That was

over a hundred years ago. It won't be alive now.'

'I guess,' he sighed. 'And I'm sure I would read about it in the history books if a Pleistocene creature started attacking people. Plus, it can't have bred. There was only one and it was a baby.'

'Well, we can be grateful for that,' Lucy said.

'Unless…' a terrible thought entered Fred's mind. 'What if history has been changed somehow? What if the future has been altered, because we let an ancient extinct creature loose on the general population?'

'Like *Jurassic Park*?' Lucy suggested. 'Oh, I forgot, that hasn't come out either. Funny how I can remember things like that so clearly.'

They reached the end of a very long street and stepped out onto a large harbour. Fred saw the distinctive roof of the Sydney Opera House in the distance. It looked like several nun's habits, all arranged on top of the building. He had no interest in going to the opera, but he had wanted to see the place. His parents had talked of taking a trip to Sydney next year. He guessed he beat them to it.

Or was he fourteen years too late?

Beyond the Sydney Opera House was a large suspension bridge, with five entwined large rings decorating it.

'The Olympics. I didn't know Australia was hosting them.' Fred said.

'I think London did once.' Lucy mused. 'Or, at least, it will do. I think I have a memory of seeing it when I was younger. For some reason, I remember the Queen parachuting into the stadium with James Bond!'

Fred laughed. 'Queen Elizabeth II?'

Lucy grinned. 'I guess it's my mind playing tricks on me. It's all fragmented, the memories in my head.'

'Was it still Roger Moore as Bond or did they get someone new?'

'No. Daniel… something. I don't really know. My brother likes Bond films. But I…'

She sighed.

'What's wrong?'

'I have a brother and I can't even remember his name.'

'At least you remember you have a brother. That's something.'

'I guess.'

They sat down on a bench, looking out over the water. It was peaceful, despite the masses of people walking up and down the Sydney Harbourfront.

He looked at the article again. 'Australia has been plagued by rumours of feral koala bears for many years now…'

'Drop bears?' Lucy asked suspiciously.

'Maybe.' He read on. 'Reports of encounters have only increased in the last decade and authorities fear another mass attack might be on the way. Citizens of Melbourne can still remember the tragic three-night killing spree in Melbourne back in 1985, where hundreds of people were slain in their homes…'

'1985,' Lucy said grimly, her face pale. 'What if there was something in that koala sanctuary, back in 1984?'

'Drop bears?' Fred asked nervously. 'But they're just local legends. Remember that news article.'

'Unless they got it wrong.' Lucy sighed. 'What if something happened after we left?'

Fred felt a cold wave of dread fill his body. His parents. His friends from school. Were they all in danger? 'We have to get back.'

Lucy nodded, staring at the time ring and gave an exasperated sigh. 'I just wish I knew how to work it.'

'Concentrate,' Fred said, putting the paper down. 'Think of my parent's basement.' He grabbed her hand. He didn't want to be stuck here if the time ring finally worked and took her back to 1985.

Lucy closed her eyes and scrunched up her face and she concentrated on taking them back. Fred watched her, holding his breath.

Nothing happened.

Lucy opened her eyes and tapped the ring angrily. 'Why won't you just work!'

She closed her eyes and tried again, but still the

ring did nothing. Eventually, she looked up and sighed, with deep frustration. Fred saw a tear trickle down her face.

'I'm so tired, Fred. I wish it would work. I wish I could take you back. I wish I knew who I really was and where I came from. I don't even remember my home, but I know I just want to get back there.'

Fred patted her hand. 'I know, I'm sorry. It's okay. You tried your best. It will work when it needs to.'

'When we're in danger, you mean?'

He frowned. 'Sorry?'

'Well, the cave, the settlers, the drop bears in the sanctuary. I know there was nothing bad at the docks. But most of the time, the time ring takes us back when we're in mortal danger.'

Fred had to agree that it was a pattern. 'Okay, well in that case, let's put ourselves in danger. Let's go looking for drop bears.'

'What do we do? Sit under a tree and see if one falls on our heads?'

'Well, if they're as dangerous as we think, surely they're going to be attracted to lots of people? The more victims, the better?'

'But it's a big city.'

'Yes, but there must be an obvious target...'

Fred looked up at the rings on the bridge and the other article on the front page.

**The city prepares for the opening
games of the 2000 Summer Olympics.**

'Lucy, if you were a horde of killer drop bears, wouldn't you find a stadium filled with thousands of people the perfect target?'

Lucy nodded. 'The ultimate all you can eat buffet.'

'Okay then. That's where we need to be. We need to get into the Sydney Olympic Stadium and make sure we're at the opening games.'

— CHAPTER EIGHTEEN —
# STOWAWAYS

The next day, Lucy stood in front of the Sydney Olympic Stadium, staring up at the huge arching roof above the entrance and wondered just how many people it would fit. Looking at the massive crowds around them and the hundreds of security guards in attendance, it was a lot.

She turned to Fred, who was reading the newspaper they had picked up earlier. It had a big section on the Olympics, which was useful if they were going to find a way inside.

'There you go,' Fred said, pointing at a particular article. 'The opening ceremony has a cast of 12,687 performers and an audience expected to reach up to 110,000. That's a lot of victims.'

Lucy shushed him. 'We don't want to draw attention and get ourselves arrested before we even get inside.'

Fred lowered his voice. 'Assuming the drop bears

are going to attack.'

'Well, it's the best we have to go on.'

They had seen three other newspapers talking about random bear attacks in the city and she had heard one man on the bus to the stadium talking to someone on the phone about "covering it up" and "adding extra security for the opening ceremony". Sydney was nervous and they were trying to hide it from the rest of the world.

'I have an idea about how we can get inside,' Fred said.

Lucy hoped he had something. They had already tried to buy tickets and the box office was sold out. There had been one man on a nearby street corner who was willing to sell tickets for ten thousand dollars apiece, but he seemed less than reputable. And even if they had been willing to believe they were real, they couldn't get that kind of money.

'Take a look at those delivery trucks over there,' he said, pointing to a troop of vehicles driving round the back of the stadium. 'If we can sneak on-board one of those, I'm sure we could find a way into the stadium.'

'Sounds dangerous, but I don't think we've got a choice.'

They pushed their way through the crowd of tourists and security guards outside the stadium, trying to remain as inconspicuous as possible. A long queue of lorries congregated beside the loading bay at the side of the stadium.

'I'm not sure how we can get inside those. What about sneaking directly through the loading bay entrance?

'Have you seen the size of those rifles?' Fred asked, pointing to the security guards at the entrance. They all carried long guns, many of them with extra body armour. They were obviously prepared for any potential threat or incursion into the stadium.

'I guess not,' Lucy mumbled.

They walked along the vehicles, searching for a way to sneak inside. But every single one of them was bolted shut. Lucy's heart fell. Fred's plan might not work after all.

The door of a lorry's cab opened ahead of them and a large, burly delivery driver with a cap stepped out, talking loudly on the phone.

'Yeah, mate. It's going to be at least three of four more hours yet. Security is crazy here. Just keep a couple of cold ones aside until I get there.'

The man continued chatting, taking another step away from the driver's cab. The door was still swung wide open.

'What do you think?' Fred suggested. 'Can we sneak inside while he's distracted?'

Lucy's heart began to race. 'What if he sees us?'

'Do we have another choice?' Fred shrugged and hurried closer to the lorry. The driver was still chatting, his back to the cab. And them.

Fred turned back. 'Come on!' he whispered. 'Now's our chance!'

Lucy bit her lip and raced after Fred. She was terrified the driver would spot them sneaking on-board, or worse, one of the security guards. But they made it inside, undetected.

There was a surprising amount of space behind the driver and passenger seat. A few boxes and a bunk bed too. Lucy guessed this man drove long haul across Australia.

'All right mate, see you later!'

Lucy looked up in alarm as the driver turned off his phone and began to walk back to his lorry.

'Quick, let's get under those blankets before he spots us!'

They grabbed two big blankets and scrambled onto the bunk bed just in time, smothering themselves as the driver climbed back on-board and slammed the side door shut.

It stank of body odour under the blankets and Lucy had to hold her breath as they waited. She could hear the creak of leather as the driver slunk back in his chair, letting out a jaunty whistle as he waited. Luckily, it didn't sound like he had spotted them.

Fred mouthed, 'Are you okay?' silently beside her. Lucy gave him a gentle nod but dared not say anything. She was trying to pay attention to what was happening outside the blanket, which was becoming increasingly harder with the sound of her own heart thudding in her chest.

'Finally!' the driver exclaimed, and she heard the ignition as he turned the engine on. There was a gentle rock as the cab moved and the lorry began to drive towards the loading bay.

After a moment, it stopped again, and Lucy heard the door swing open.

'Stadium security. Identification please.'

Lucy held her breath. If the security guards searched the rest of the cab, they would be spotted in an instant.

The wait to be discovered felt like an eternity. She couldn't make out what was happening, but she dared not lift the blanket to see.

'Okay, seems in order. Make your way to loading point seven.'

The driver didn't seem to respond, but the door slammed, and she heard the ignition again. The lorry began to move. Lucy assumed that it was moving inside the loading bay. It must be large. But then, the stadium was big enough to hold over a 100,000 people.

Lucy had almost got used to the smell by the time

the lorry came to a stop. She heard the driver turn the ignition key, open the cab door and step outside. Lucy gingerly peeled the blanket back to make sure the coast was clear.

'Follow me,' she muttered to Fred, crawling off the bunk towards the driver's seat and the open door. Together they peered over the top of the large windscreen and saw the driver talking to a couple of loading bay workers. One of which was ticking off something on a clipboard. A security guard walked by in the distance.

'I think we need to wait just a little longer,' Lucy said quietly. 'They'll spot us if we climb out now.'

'I agree,' Fred concurred.

Finally, the driver and the two workers moved off towards the back of the lorry. There was a loud clang of what Lucy assumed was the doors of the big container on the back being opened.

Ahead of them, the security guard vanished through a large hangar bay doorway into another part of the stadium.

'Now!' she whispered.

Lucy scrambled down the big steps out of the driver's cab and her feet landed with a thud on the concrete floor. Fred was right behind her.

'Over there, behind those packing crates!' Fred whispered, pointing to huge columns of crates that reached almost to the high ceiling of the loading bay.

Lucy grabbed his hand, and they ran. They made it to the packing crates in one piece. When they were confident that they hadn't been spotted, they began moving slowly through the hangar bay, hidden behind deliveries supplies, crates, boxes and parked vehicles. More and more lorries made their way into the stadium. Despite the vigilance of security everywhere, there was enough commotion happening that they didn't attract any attention.

Eventually, they found their way out of the large hangar bays and climbed a steep staircase up to the next level. They stepped out onto a narrow corridor with large glass windows looking out onto the stadium.

'It's huge!' Lucy said with a gasp, staring at the wide-open arena and rows and rows of seats rising all the way to the roof.

'I can see why it holds that many people,' Fred said. 'I've never seen a stadium this big.'

Lucy thought she might have been in a stadium once, maybe to watch an event – a concert perhaps? It had felt as big as this.

'We've got to find somewhere to hide until the games begin,' Fred said, leading her down the corridor. There was no one about, though there was plenty of commotion down in the arena as people prepared for the start of the Olympic games.

They came to a door that read *storage*. 'What

about this?' Fred suggested. He didn't wait for an answer. He was already turning the handle.

The room inside was larger than she expected, filled with boxes. 'I guess it's as good a place as anywhere for two stowaways to wait.'

They snuck inside and closed the door. Fred looked at her hesitantly. 'What happens if the drop bears don't attack the opening games?'

Lucy didn't really have an answer. It was the best guess they had. There was no other place in the city that would have this many potential victims all in one place. She yawned.

But she couldn't sleep. If she was right, the drop bears were coming. She wanted nothing more than to be wrong. Almost as much as she wanted to go home.

# CHAPTER NINETEEN

# THE OPENING CEREMONY

The stadium was packed to the rafters, and Fred was sure he had never seen so many people in one place. Many wore bright colours, painted rings on their faces. Everywhere he turned there was the bustle of excitement as the stadium waited for the games to begin.

Once people had started filling into the arena for the opening ceremony, it hadn't been hard to blend in. They didn't have to get past the ticket booths and security checks at the entrances to the stadium and it had been easy to become part of the crowd.

'Shall we get something to eat?' he suggested.

Lucy frowned. 'Haven't we got more pressing matters to concern ourselves with?'

'You said it yourself, we have no idea if and when the drop bears will attack. Besides, the opening ceremony is apparently four hours long and I haven't had anything since lunch. I'm famished.'

As if on cue, his stomach rumbled.

'Okay,' Lucy nodded, a grin forming on her face. 'A burger would be nice.'

'There's a Macca's over there.'

'A what?'

'McDonalds, don't you have them in the future?' Fred asked.

'Yes, but we don't call them that,' Lucy replied.

'Must be an Australian thing.' Fred pushed Lucy towards a long queue of people grabbing food and refreshments before the opening ceremony began. They didn't have much change left from the twenty dollars Lucy had found – only enough for a cheese burger and milkshake each.

They found a free bench to sit on and devoured their dinner hungrily.

Eventually the crowds began to make their way to their seats. Without tickets of their own, Fred and Lucy hung back.

Finally, there were enough people inside. They made their move.

A large woman blocked their path. 'Tickets please?'

Fred froze, unsure what to say. But Lucy stepped forward, slurping her milkshake. 'Hi, yeah. Our parents are inside. We went back for drinks, but we forgot to bring our tickets with us. Can you let us in please?'

The attendant eyed her suspiciously. 'Your parents are inside?'

'Well, not the same parents obviously?' she said quickly. 'Do we look alike? My mum works with Fred's mum here, and we all came here together with Phillipa, who's our cousin from Melbourne, and Fred's uncle Dougie, who you know, doesn't get out much, and…'

The woman held up her hands to stop her. 'Okay, okay. No need to tell me your life story. Why didn't your parents come back out with you?'

'I'm fifteen and Fred's sixteen!' Lucy said indignantly. 'We don't normally need to be accompanied by an adult just to buy a drink!'

Lucy stuck her hand on her hip and slurped her drink, waiting for a response.

'Okay, that's fine. But it's very busy. Next time tell an adult they must accompany you. I wouldn't want you both to get lost.'

'Yeah, thanks!' Lucy said with a fake smile and stepped through into the arena. Fred followed her with a look of bewilderment.

'That was amazing!' he said with a gasp.

'Well, it's all about having conviction. Come on, let's find somewhere we can hang out.'

They scanned the rows and rows of seats, looking for somewhere to watch the opening ceremony and look out for drop bears. Knowing that the stadium was sold out, they couldn't take someone's seat. Or they'd risk being thrown out.

Luckily, they found a small enclave between two blocks of seating. They didn't have great views of the arena below, but they were mostly out of sight. It would have to do for now.

Fred noticed several attendants scanning the seating areas, checking for tickets. He looked at Lucy nervously. 'What do we do? They're coming this way.'

'Come with me.' Lucy said, grabbing his hand.

She led him right past one attendant, marching between two rows of seats, much to the frustration of a few people already seated.

'Just pretend we're walking back to our seats,' she told him.

By the time the lights had faded, and the arena went dark, they had passed three blocks of seating and the attendants seemed to have dispersed. Lucy spotted two vacant seats close to the front.

'I'm guessing whoever brought them should have been seated by now,' she told him.

'If we see anyone moving towards us, we can just move on,' Fred replied and followed her to the seats.

They weren't seated next to each other. There was a young woman with bright pink hair between the two empty seats, but she didn't pay them attention as they sat down. Fred waited for someone to tap him on the shoulder and explain he was sat in their seat, but no one seemed to care.

The opening ceremony began.

Fred watched excitedly as a man on a horse, holding a white banner with the five Olympic rings, trotted into the main arena to the fanfare of music. He was followed by several more men and women on horseback, all carrying the white banners with rings. It was an impressive sight, and he was grateful to get the chance to experience it.

Fred had been too exhausted to really contemplate the many wonders and dangers of the last couple of days. He was a real time traveller! He had witnessed prehistoric creatures, spies and suffragettes, and the settling of modern Australia from Europe. These were experiences straight out of the history books – or one of Matty's epic sci-fi novels. He could hardly believe it was real.

And now he was here in the future, watching an epic Olympic games opening ceremony. It was exciting. He really hoped the drop bears didn't attack.

The horsemen gave an impressive series of displays on the arena floor below before dispersing to the side as a giant white banner, with bold colours and the word G'DAY rippled down over the arena. The crowd went wild. Fred rose from his seat and applauded with everyone else. All his exhaustion and worries were gone as he was caught up in the moment.

As he sat down, still clapping, a multi-coloured dressed brass band began to play. The music filled the stadium, and he was caught up once again in the cheers from the crowd. He looked to Lucy, sat beyond the pink-haired lady, and grinned. She grinned back.

A voice rang out over the stadium, speaking in French, which he didn't understand. But as a white light fell on the section of the seating, high over the stadium floor, it was followed by a man's voice.

'Ladies and gentlemen. Will you please welcome his excellency, the honourable Sir William Deane, the Governor-General of Australia, and the President of the International Olympic Committee Juan Antonio Samaranch.'

Trumpets blared and one of the two men that had been introduced, waved to the crowd. Fred raised his hands to cheers again.

A piercing scream rang through the stadium. Then another and another.

The trumpet sound turned to a wailing screech and Fred saw what was happening. Something large and furry had latched onto the trumpet and was trying to attack the player. Across the arena, the man that had been waving fell forward as something dark landed on his face.

The crowd broke into a panic as screams rippled through the stadium. More creatures appeared, dropping into the crowd from the open roof of the stadium. Fred saw one land and attack a man three seats away.

It looked like an oversized koala, and its claws were slashing furiously at the man as he crumped to the ground. Its beady black eyes shone in the light of the arena and liquid-like goo dripped from its mouth.

It was completely feral.

It was a drop bear.

Hundreds of drop bears fell into the stadium and Fred sat frozen, staring in horror at the chaos unfolding around him. On the stadium floor, poor riders were being attacked by drop bears, as their horses galloped wilding across the arena. People were jumping out of their seats, some stampeding for the exits while the drop bears attacked the crowd.

'Fred!'

Over the screams of the crowd, he heard Lucy's panicked voice. He rose from his seat and scrambled towards her.

She wasn't being attacked, but there was no mistaking the glow of the time ring on her hand.

Desperately, Fred lunged towards her, but the woman with the pink hair blocked his path. Fred slammed against her in shock and fell back into his seat, realising that he was going to be trapped here.

He really wished Lucy hadn't been right.

Lucy pushed the woman aside and reached out to grab him. He pulled himself up and held out his hand. His finger almost reached her when the woman pushed herself between them, trying to get out of her seat. The last thing Fred saw was the ring growing brighter on Lucy's hand.

And then she vanished before his very eyes…

— CHAPTER TWENTY —

# THE DROP BEARS ATTACK

Lucy could still hear the panicked screams of the stadium as the flash of light faded and she fell onto hard, warm concrete. It took her a moment to catch her breath. The palms of her hands stung from where they had hit the ground and she carefully picked up bits of stone and dirt from them as she staggered to her feet.

Only to be greeted by another white flash of light.

It took her a moment to realise that she was standing in the road. A car was coming right towards her, the driver honking their horn from somewhere behind the car's headlamps. Lucy begun to panic.

The car swerved to a halt just in front of her and Lucy caught her breath, trembling with shock as she staggered out of the road.

She was confused by what was happening. The

time ring had brought them to several different locations before, but never one that had immediately put them in danger.

Fred!

As she reached the pavement, Lucy frantically scanned the road for any sign of her friend. The driver that had almost hit her shouted something rude in her direction and drove off. Traffic was already moving in the opposite direction, and it was hard to make out what was going on because it was night.

Someone moved at the far side of the road and Lucy's heart leapt in the hope that it was Fred.

No. It was…the woman with the pink hair that had been sat in the stadium between her and Fred.

Lucy couldn't see anyone else on the pavement and the traffic was already running smoothly. It took her a moment to realise what the water in her eyes was. She was crying.

She let go of the breath she had been holding and realised that Fred wasn't here. In the chaos, the woman from the future must have touched her as the time ring activated, which meant he was still there. In a stadium with the drop bears.

She sniffed, wiping away the tears and tapped furiously at the time ring on her hand.

'Take me back!' she screamed. 'Take me back to Fred!'

It didn't matter how dangerous it was. She couldn't leave him there.

But the time ring didn't activate. With a scream of frustration, Lucy ripped it from her finger and was about to toss it into the road before she stopped herself.

No. She couldn't. Not if there was a chance that she might be able to travel forward and save him. It was also still her only chance of getting back to her own life.

Lucy put the ring back on, wiped the rest of the tears from her cheeks and took a deep breath. She had to be strong. She had to find a way to make the time ring work and see if she could avert the catastrophe in the year 2000, and maybe, maybe even find a way home.

Alone.

She took a deep breath to calm the rising sense of panic in her stomach. She didn't know where she was. *When* she was.

Lucy froze. Something *growled* in the darkness.

She looked up towards the streetlamp hanging over her and saw the shadow of a creature swinging off the light.

A drop bear!

Lucy screamed as the drop bear leapt towards her, claws spread out. She jumped back, barely missing the swipe of the drop bear's claws. It was slightly bigger than a koala bear, with beady black eyes and long, black claws nestled on the ends of its soft, furry paws. If it wasn't making that sound, she would have almost described it as cute.

The drop bear scrambled off into the distance and Lucy followed cautiously, watching as it climbed up the side of a tree and vanished over a tall wall.

Something about that wall felt oddly familiar.

There was the rustle in the trees beyond the wall and she realised where she was. She was standing outside the koala sanctuary!

Had she come back to 1984?

A woman walked down the street. Lucy took a deep breath and approached her.

'Hi!'

The woman froze, giving her a suspicious look. 'Hello?'

'Bit of an odd question, but what year is this?'

The woman looked at her like she was mad. '1985. Why? Are you lost?'

'Er, no. That's great, thanks.'

1985? Perhaps she had arrived back in the present… or at least the present she had spent the last few weeks in with Fred.

If this was the koala sanctuary, then she had to be in Melbourne, near to the restaurant where they had fled from Ashna. The time ring had brought her back to where they had started.

But what was she going to do now? If there were drop bears here, then…

She remembered the newspaper report.

Reports of attacks have only increased in the last decade and authorities fear another mass attack might be on the way. Citizens of Melbourne can still remember the tragic three-night killing spree in Melbourne back in 1985, where hundreds of people were slaughtered in their homes.

Was this where she was now, the start of a deadly attack? Were the drop bears here? She had to warn someone. But who? Who would believe her?

Marvin!

She no longer trusted the book shop owner, but she knew he was most likely to believe her story. He might even know something about the time ring. Maybe he could help her go forward in time and save Fred from the drop bears?

The trees rustled beyond the wall of the koala bear sanctuary. Lucy looked up nervously as the sound of breaking branches, rustling leaves and low growls filled the night air. Something was coming towards the edge of the sanctuary.

There was more than one drop bear in there.

Lucy began to run. The noise was getting louder, and the trees were moving violently. She ran to the nearest bus stop and realised that she didn't have any money on her. So, she kept running, down the street, past cars and lorries and saw the lights of the restaurant up ahead. The same restaurant where Ashna had brought Matty and saved his parents.

If nothing else, she could hide out in there.

Behind her she heard a scream and the screech of a car. Lucy looked over her shoulder as at least twenty bears clambered over the wall of the sanctuary and poured into the street. One car swerved to avoid them and ended up crashing into another. The traffic quickly ground to a halt and the growling drop bears began clambering over the vehicles with the terrified passengers still inside.

The drop bears were attacking Melbourne and she was powerless to stop it.

Lucy ran into the restaurant, startling the diners inside. She stood at the doorway, sweating, panting, looking awkwardly at the faces staring in her direction. Some people looked at her angrily, others confused.

'You've got to, got…' She gasped.

One of the waitresses rushed towards her, her face like thunder. 'Out you go! This is a respectable establishment, and we won't have—'

'They're coming!' Lucy interrupted her.

The waitress frowned. 'Who is coming?'

'The drop bears!'

One of the diners at a nearby table laughed. 'Drop bears? Yeah, right. Is there a Yeti in the toilet too?'

Before she could respond, the main window overlooking the street exploded in a shower of glass. Diners screamed, scrambling from their tables. Lucy turned and gasped in horror as four drop bears leapt onto the tables.

'I, I told, you…' she mumbled desperately.

The waitress looked at the bears in horror and addressed the terrified diners. 'The restaurant is closed. Please make your way to the back. You can exit through the kitchen!'

The diners made a panicked rush towards the back of the restaurant. One of the drop bears landed on a diner's back and slashed at his jacket with its claws. Lucy grabbed a vase from a nearby stand and threw it at the bear, knocking it from its victim. The man shoved his way past Lucy without even a thank you.

Three more drop bears scrambled into the restaurant. Outside, Lucy could hear screams, cars crashing to a halt and even an explosion.

The waitress grabbed her arm. 'Come on!'

Lucy followed quickly as more drop bears filled the restaurant. The last of the diners were pushing their way through the swinging doors into the kitchen.

They were almost there when a table fell over, blocking their path. Lucy and the waitress stumbled back, looking for an escape. Three snarling drop bears clambered over the table towards them, their beady eyes gleaming. She turned and saw three more circling from behind.

They were trapped!

# CHAPTER TWENTY-ONE

# THE DROP BEARS ATTACK AGAIN

'Where am I?'

Fred opened his eyes, and his head begin to throb. He sat up, rubbing his head and took in his surroundings. He wasn't in the stadium anymore, but a busy street at night. Cars rushed past, and three people were hovering over him.

None of them were Lucy.

Perhaps he had been knocked unconscious during the attack on the stadium. Had someone carried him outside? Was Lucy okay or had she gone to another time and place without him?

'What happened?'

One of the people knelt beside him, a man with big friendly eyes and a warm smile. 'You hit your head pretty hard there, son. You're lucky we pulled you out of the road when we did.'

The road? 'How did I get here?'

'Will someone tell me what is going on?!' someone else, a woman, screamed.

The kindly man gave Fred a pat on the shoulder and stood up. 'Listen! Stay calm and let's call an ambulance to get you checked out.'

'I don't need to stay calm!' The woman shouted angrily. 'I want to know how I got here! One minute we're in the games, the next, I'm stood here in the middle of the road with two kids, and nearly got myself killed!'

Fred looked up and blinked in surprise. The pink-haired woman! 'It's you!'

The pink-haired woman glared at him. 'Yes, it's me! Do *you* know what happened?'

Fred pulled himself onto his feet, aided by the man. 'Where's the stadium? Were we taken outside?'

The man shook his head. 'There's no stadium around here, young man.'

'Then how…' Fred rubbed his head again and looked at the woman. 'What do you remember?'

The pink-haired woman gave him an exasperated sigh. 'We were in the stadium, watching the opening games. Then these bears started attacking the crowd. You grabbed my arm. I fell onto that girl with the curly hair, and then there was some kind of flash of light. The next thing I know, we're stood in the middle of traffic, you've hit the ground and knocked yourself out, and I had to drag you to safety before we were hit by a car.'

Fred felt a surge of hope. 'The girl, is she here?'

The pink-haired woman shrugged. 'I don't know. She ran off. I was too preoccupied with getting you to safety. Thank you very much.'

'Yeah, thanks.' Fred said. He wanted to show more gratitude, but he was more preoccupied with what had happened to Lucy and where they were now. Had the three of them travelled through time together?

He turned to the kindly man. 'Where are we? What city is this? What year is this?'

The man shook his head. 'You really did hit your head hard, didn't you? I should go and call for an ambulance.'

'Please, just tell me!' Fred pleaded.

'We're in Melbourne.'

'No, we're not!' The woman interjected. 'We're in Sydney.'

'And what year is this?'

'1985.'

The woman laughed. 'Okay, now you're being ridiculous!'

Fred couldn't help but feel his heart swell. Was he home? Was Lucy here too? Why had they been separated? He had to find her!

Any thoughts on what to do next was interrupted

by a terrified scream. A car screeched to a halt in the street as loads of small, furry creatures clambered over a tall wall across from them.

Fred realised what this place was. He had been here with Lucy before…

The koala sanctuary.

'It's them!' the woman screeched.

Fred gulped. Drop bears.

All the cars in the road came to a halt, two crashing into the side of each other as the drivers slammed on their breaks. The drop bears climbed over the vehicles, scratching at the windows to try and get inside.

'We have to hide!' Fred said uneasily, his head still throbbing.

'But…'

The man didn't get a chance to say any more as one of the drop bears leapt onto his back from a nearby car. The pink-haired woman ran off, while Fred and the second man attempted to try and pull the drop bear away.

The drop bear reached out and scratched at the second man's face with its sharp claws, its big, black eyes glaring at them.

Behind them, a lorry smashed into the side of a car and exploded. The drop bears went wild as people desperately tried to escape their vehicles.

The three nights of carnage in Melbourne. This

was what that Sydney newspaper had been talking about. It meant people were going to die and he had no way of stopping it.

Fred pulled the backpack off his shoulders and whacked it against the side of the drop bear. It fell off and went off in search of easier prey. The injured man staggered to his feet, supported by the second man.

'Thank you,' the man gasped, in obvious pain. 'Quick, get inside while you can.'

Fred didn't need to be told twice. He followed the two men into a nearby shop where several people were already barricading themselves in. Out on the street, a second explosion destroyed another car and people were running screaming. More and more drop bears climbed over the wall of the koala sanctuary.

How many were there? Fifty? A hundred?

Where was Lucy? He couldn't stay in the shop while she might be in danger. He had to find her and then call his parents. They would be worried sick. Worse still, they might be in danger too. If this lasted three nights, the drop bears would rampage across the entire city of Melbourne. No one was safe.

One of the drop bears slammed against the shop window, its claws scratching furiously as it tried to find a way in. A couple of the people in the shop were crying, others were huddled in the aisles, many dealing with the wounds that had already been inflicted upon them. The man with the kind smile looked like he was in pain, but his friend was helping tend to his wounds. Luckily, he was going to live.

'What are they?' one of the men inside asked, as three more drop bears scratched and clawed at the window.

'Drop bears!' Fred told him firmly, looking around for something that he could use as makeshift weapon.

'Drop bears aren't real,' the man said.

The shop keeper stepped out from behind the till, a baseball bat in hand. 'They look real enough to me.'

The shop door swung open as two panicked people rushed inside for safety. Before they could slam the door shut, one of the drop bears broke through. There were several screams and whimpers, but the shopkeeper stepped forward, bat in hand. The drop bear lunged at him, but the shopkeeper swung the bat and struck the creature, sending it crashing into a stack of cans.

'Not in my shop, you don't!' he shouted.

Fred ran down the aisles, looking for a weapon. A baseball bat would have been ideal, but he did discover a couple of sturdy wooden brooms in the household cleaning aisle. He grabbed one. It was solid enough to use as a quarterstaff and the base of the broom, a hammer. A couple of wooden kitchen mallets also looked handy and he shoved them inside his backpack.

Behind him, the shop window exploded. Several drop bears burst in. Amid the screams and panic, several of the people inside grabbed tins, boxes, and anything else that was remotely solid and began throwing them at the creatures. The shop owner with the baseball bat whacked several of the drop bears back out of reach.

There was no chance of getting out that way. Fred found a back door leading to a stock room, left the spare bit of change that he hadn't been able to spend in 2000 on a shelf for the weapons, and hoped the shopkeeper would find it. Broom in hand, he moved quickly through the stock room and found a back door leading into an alley beyond.

Even though the sounds of screams, explosions and general chaos could be heard nearby, the alley itself was quiet. It was pitch black too, but the dark was the least of his problems. Gritting his teeth, Fred ran along the back, searching for a way out.

As he left the alley, people ran past, screaming. But they seemed to be running away from the danger of the drop bears. There were no drop bears in sight.

Fred ran across the road and spotted a drop bear climbing up a lamppost. It saw him and growled, ready to pounce. Fred gripped the broom and readied himself for the attack.

The drop bear leapt, and Fred swung. The base of the broom struck the drop bear and it fell back, wounded. Realising that Fred wasn't quite such easy prey, it scampered off back towards the rest of its kin.

Up ahead, a restaurant was under attack from several drop bears. Fred thought it was the same restaurant where that strange woman with the glowing green eyes had taken Matty.

The windows were broken, tables and chairs were upturned, and two people were inside, surrounded by several of the creatures.

Fred gasped. One of them was Lucy!

He charged towards the restaurant, broom swinging. He knocked two drop bears clear and leapt over broken glass through the open doorway. Another drop bear charged him, and he swung, the broom knocking it into a table.

Lucy saw him and gasped.

'Fred, you're *here*! How?'

'Good to see you too,' he said with a grin. 'Now let's get out of here!'

— CHAPTER TWENTY-TWO —
# THE THREE RULES

Lucy couldn't believe Fred was here. She had a million questions, but no time to ask them. Before she knew it, she was running out of the restaurant with Fred and the waitress into a world of chaos.

A car had been flipped over and was on fire. Luckily, there wasn't anyone inside. She could hear screams in the distance, but it looked as if most of the people in this part of the city had already run for safety.

Unfortunately, for them, they weren't alone. Three drop bears swung from a nearby lamppost and scurried towards them, growling as they bared their fangs.

'Here, take this!' Fred said, handing her a wooden mallet from his rucksack. He was carrying a large broom, which she presumed he was using as a weapon.

Lucy took the mallet nervously. It was quite heavy, and she would need to get close to hit one of the bears. Fred, however, was already swinging the broom wildly in front of him, knocking one drop bear back as it got too close.

'We can't fight these things!' the waitress snapped. 'We've got to run!'

Lucy was inclined to agree. A broom and a mallet weren't enough against these vicious, feral creatures.

'Come on!' she yelled, starting to run in the opposite direction. Fred brushed another one back and joined them as they ran down the street in search of safety.

Luckily for them, the drop bears weren't as fast as they were. In a couple of minutes, they found themselves on a deserted side street. They could still hear the occasional scream in the distance, but they had passed the worst of it.

There were lights from houses along the street, but outside was empty. It was oddly quiet, as if the whole world had suddenly held its breath, waiting for the next thing to happen.

'What now?' Lucy asked.

'We need to hide and then call the police,' the waitress said firmly.

'I need to call Mum and Dad,' Fred said anxiously. 'Let them know we're okay.'

'And yours?' the waitress asked, turning to Lucy.

Lucy hesitated. 'They're, er, out of town. I'm staying with Fred's family.'

'Okay,' the waitress said, seemingly convinced. 'Let's keep going. My flat is only a couple of streets away.'

Lucy nodded. She wasn't sure how close to Mentone this part of Melbourne was. Right now, finding a place to regroup and think was the best option.

Lucy's legs ached as they walked, but she was used to feeling tired by now. It seemed like months since she had slept in a bed. Even the camper bed in Fred's basement would do. It had probably only been a couple of days since the museum, but everything felt different when you were jumping back and forth through time.

They passed a couple of police cars, sirens blaring as they raced towards the drop bears' attack. Lucy hoped they might be able to do something.

But what? They were only animals? Did they deserve to be killed? Could they be locked up, in a nature reserve, like the koalas? She hated the idea that they might be caged. But then, they were too dangerous to be left free to roam across Australia.

When they reached the waitress' flat, Lucy's head felt heavy with deep, forbidding thoughts. She was glad they were back in 1985, but they might as well be back in 1895 again. This wasn't her home and there was just a great a danger here as there had been on any of their travels.

The waitress (Lucy realised she still didn't know her name) showed them inside the small studio apartment. It was one large room with a separate bathroom to the rear. A tiny kitchen, a bed, a sofa, TV, VCR, and book stands. There was also a large stack of videos by the TV and posters in frames on the wall. Lucy thought it looked kind of cool.

'Right, the bathroom's over there if you need to wash up.' The waitress said. 'I'll call the police, though it looks like they might already be dealing with it.'

Fred went to the bathroom, while Lucy sat on the sofa, waiting as the waitress made a call. It wasn't long before she hung up.

'I can't get though. I guess everyone has the same idea.' She sighed, sitting down next to Lucy. 'Are you okay? You were very brave back there. Both of you.'

Lucy smiled, awkwardly. 'I was just trying to save people.'

'You were very brave.' The waitress repeated, smiling.

'Thanks. I'm Lucy,'

'Emily.'

'Hi, Emily,' Lucy said, shaking her hand. 'What now?'

'I don't know,' Emily said with a sigh. 'What were those things?'

'Drop bears,' Fred said grimly, stepping out of the bathroom.

Emily gave them an awkward laugh. 'Drop bears? They're just a myth.'

'Feral koala bears that attack people?' Fred replied. 'They looked real to me.'

Emily sighed. 'I can't argue with that. Did you want to try your mum and dad?'

'Oh yeah, right.' Fred said, heading for the phone. Lucy and Emily waited as he dialled and waited for his parents to pick up.

'Mum! It's Fred, Yes, I know… it's…what?'

'What is it?' Lucy asked nervously.

Fred put his hand over the received. 'We've been gone two days. They're worried sick.' He returned to the call. 'Listen, Mum. It's okay, we're all right. Lucy is with me and… Mum? Mum?'

'What now?' Lucy asked.

Fred shook his head. 'The call cut off.' He put the receiver down and then tried dialling again. 'I'm not getting a dial tone.'

Emily frowned and rushed over to the phone, taking it from Fred. She tried a couple of times. 'You're right. I think it's our end. The phone line has gone dead.'

'Or it's been cut,' Lucy sighed. 'The drop bears.'

'Which means they're getting close.' Fred groaned. 'We've got to do something.'

'Something?' Emily said. 'You don't have to do anything. You stay here with me until it's safe.'

'Nowhere is safe with the drop bears around,' Fred said, grabbing his broom weapon. 'We need to go now. Try and get across the city before we're cut off.'

'Okay, but let's think about this,' Lucy replied. That mallet you gave me, isn't going to do me any good. We need—'

'Vegemite!' Fred exclaimed.

Lucy frowned. 'Vegemite? What are you going to do? Throw jars of it at them?'

'No, we're going to slather ourselves in it.'

Emily laughed. 'You want to slather yourself in Vegemite?'

'Yes! The three rules, remember?'

Lucy didn't know whether to laugh or throw her arms up in exasperation. 'You're not serious?'

'Why not? We've got nothing left to lose.'

'Except our lives!' Lucy snapped.

'Well, yeah… but hear me out. A few days ago, we thought drop bears were a myth. But now, drop bears are rampaging through Melbourne. So, if they are real, then maybe there's some truth to the rules too.'

'Wait,' Emily said loudly. 'You're talking about

covering yourself in vegemite, talking in an Australian accent and calling everyone Bruce? That's not a sensible plan, young man.'

'It's like *Gremlins*!' Fred replied. 'We have rampaging monsters tearing through the streets. And there are three rules you have to follow.'

'This isn't a movie,' Emily said firmly.

'Maybe it's exactly like a movie. We've got nothing to lose from trying.'

'Except our lives,' Lucy repeated herself flatly.

'I wish you would stop saying that!' Fred growled.

'Perhaps you should listen to your friend,' Emily added.

'I'm going,' Fred told them adamantly. 'I need to get back to my mum and dad. They're worried sick. And I've got a lot of city to cover.' He looked at Lucy, his face stern. 'Are you with me?'

Lucy looked at those big, worried eyes and nodded. 'Yes, I'm with you.'

'You're both crazy!' Emily exclaimed.

'Oh, we're completely crazy,' Fred said. 'But we can't stay here. Now, do you have any Vegemite?'

'You're really serious about this?'

'We are,' Lucy said, stepping beside her friend. 'I know the whole Bruce thing sounds crazy, but maybe there's some truth in all of this too. For all we know, drop bears are allergic to Vegemite. If we're covered in the stuff, they might leave us alone.'

'Yeah, she's right,' Fred added. 'And we're not crazy enough to attack them. We're trying to get away from them. But if it offers even the slightest bit of protection…'

Emily obviously realised she wasn't going to talk them out of their plan. She threw up her arms, sighed and marched over to the kitchen cupboard.

'It's a good job I like Vegemite,' she said, taking out a small jar and opening it. 'But there's not much here for a good slathering, I'm afraid. I'm almost out.'

Lucy took the jar disappointedly. 'Okay, we'll use it sparingly, like war paint.'

'War paint?' Emily muttered under her breath, but she didn't press the issue. 'I suppose you'll want to take my broom, too? This young man here seemed to use his quite well fending off the bears.'

'Thank you,' Lucy said with a smile. She didn't fancy getting into hand-to-hand combat with a drop bear with just a wooden mallet.

Soon, they were prepared. Brooms in hand, their arms, legs and faces covered in lines of sticky, dark Vegemite. It really did look like war paint.

Emily led them back downstairs to the main entrance to the block of flats. Fortunately, the street outside was empty. Police sirens rang in the air, and they could see smoke from a fire not far in the distance.

'Good luck,' Emily said from the door. 'I hope you get back to your parents.'

'Thanks,' Lucy said. 'You're very brave too.'

Emily smiled and closed the door. Lucy looked down the empty street and took a deep breath. 'Which way?'

'Right, I guess. It's away from the carnage.' He looked at Lucy and smirked. 'Oh, by the way. You stink of Vegemite.'

Lucy sniggered. 'So, do you!'

# CHAPTER TWENTY-THREE

# FRED'S PLAN

'And then when I woke up, you were gone,' Fred finished, walking alongside Lucy down the abandoned street. There was no one about. Everyone must have been hiding from the drop bears.

'I'm so glad you're here.' Lucy sighed. 'I was so worried the drop bears were going to get you at the stadium.'

'So was I,' Fred said, holding out the broom in front of him defensively. They had walked down three streets and there were no signs of the drop bears. But he had to be alert.

'So, what's the plan?' Lucy asked. 'Find a bus or a train and try and make it back to your parents?'

'I guess so. You see those lights? They look like shops and bars.'

They raced ahead, but soon wished they hadn't. As they ran towards a row of brightly lit bars and restaurants, they discovered that most of the establishments had already been abandoned. There were upturned chairs and tables lying in the street and a car on fire, that had crashed into a shop window.

'The drop bears must have been here already,' Fred said with a sigh.

'Which means they're spreading through the city,' Lucy said. 'We must be at least a mile or two from the sanctuary by now.'

'Stay alert,' Fred said, holding out the broom.

A scream came from up ahead, somewhere out of sight, but Fred gritted his teeth and tried to remain calm.

A police car raced down the street, sirens blaring, followed by a fire engine. They knocked the fallen chairs out of their path and kept moving. A woman ran out of one of the bars, gave them a panicked look and kept on running. She must have encountered the drop bears already.

'Fred!'

Fred turned and saw Lucy was still behind him, staring at one of the restaurants they had passed. She looked terrified and he quickly realised why. Six drop bears were climbing out of the wreckage and their beady eyes were fixed upon them.

'I'm not so sure the rules are going to work, Fred,' Lucy said nervously.

Fred wasn't convinced either. 'Just remember the

accent when you start calling them Bruce.'

The first drop bears scrambled towards them.

'G'Day, Bruce!' Fred yelled in the thickest Aussie accent he could muster. The first drop bear paused. Was it because the rules worked or because it was confused why Fred wasn't screaming?

'G'Day, Bruce! G'Day, Bruce!' Lucy yelled at two other drop bears.

'What kind of accent was that?!' Fred cried. 'Australian, not Irish?'

'I don't know how to do an Australian accent!' Lucy groaned, thought about *Neighbours*, and tried again.

'G'Day, Bruce!'

'G'Day Bruce!'

'G'Day, Bruce! Fancy 'aving a barbie?'

'A what?' Fred exclaimed.

Lucy looked at him sheepishly. 'You know, Australians call it a barbie, well Karl Kennedy does anyway. As opposed to a barbeque?'

Fred shook his head and gingerly took a step forward, broom ready. He hoped they could smell the Vegemite. He stank of it. 'G'Day, Bruce!'

The closest drop bear was having none of it. It growled and leapt onto the flat edge of the broom. It was heavier than Fred thought it would be and he almost dropped it as he tried to shake it off. Lucy had to knock it off with her broom. She swung round and hit another drop bear as it attacked.

'I don't think it's working!' Lucy screamed. 'G'Day, Bruce! 'G'day, Bruce!'

'G'Day, Bruce!' Fred yelled at the top of his lungs, but it didn't stop them from coming. Soon, all six drop bears circled around them, ready to attack.

But then they hesitated.

'The Vegemite?' Lucy asked meekly.

Fred shrugged. 'Maybe.' He took a step closer to the nearest drop bear. 'Don't like the smell, do yer?'

'Okay, I think we need to get out of here,' Lucy cried.

'Agreed. On three we make a run for it. One, two, three, run!'

They ran for the biggest gap between the drop bears. One leapt towards Lucy, but she was ready, swiping it back with her broom like some mighty battle axe. Fred swung the other way, knocking one drop bear aside, then another.

But it didn't stop them coming. Fred and Lucy ran, the six drop bears scrambling along the ground. A couple leapt towards a line of trees and began swinging from one branch to the next.

'I don't think I'm ever going to watch *Gremlins* again!' Lucy yelled as they kept running.

Fred saw the bright lights up ahead of a cinema and gasped. 'I've got a brilliant idea!'

'We cover ourselves in jam and speak Klingon in

a Norwegian accent?' Lucy yelled back.

'No! We lead them into the cinema and blow them up! Just like in *Gremlins*!'

'That's a terrible idea!'

'Well, do you have a better one?'

Lucy didn't answer. Up ahead, a car exploded in flames and several people began running in their direction. He quickly realised why. More drop bears were hunting them, climbing over the walls of buildings, abandoned cars and trees. And behind them, even more drop bears were closing in.

They were trapped.

'We're not getting out of this, are we?' Lucy cried.

Fred wished he could give her some comfort. 'I don't know, Lucy. Maybe we try and hide in the cinema. And if we can lure them in, maybe we could trap them inside.'

'I'm not blowing up a cinema. This isn't *Gremlins*!'

'I know that!' he snapped back. She was angry and scared. He was angry and scared too. But he didn't have a better idea. 'If we can lure them in though, maybe we can barricade the doors?'

Suddenly a police car screeched to a halt behind them. The nearest drop bears flocked towards the car as a policeman and policewoman got out, holding guns. But before they could fire, the drop bears were on them, forcing them back into the car. The creatures ripped the siren off the top of the car and began scratching at the windows.

Lucy shoved a drop bear away with her broom. 'Okay, your idea is the best we've got. Let's go!'

Fred didn't need to be told twice. They ran towards the cinema.

Even more drop bears burst through the swing doors at the entrance of the cinema, blocking their path. Fred staggered to a halt and took Lucy's free hand in theirs.

'I don't think my plan is going to work at all!'

Once again, they were trapped. And this time, there were more drop bears then she could count. They had no way of escaping…

# CHAPTER TWENTY-FOUR

# A SURPRISE ALLY

As the drop bears closed in from all directions, Lucy began to panic. She wished the time ring would take her out of here and drag Fred and her across time. But to where?

A sudden whirring filled the air above them. Lucy looked up and saw two large military helicopters rising over the rooftops of the city. On the street, several jeeps raced towards the cinema, navigating their way through panicked crowds of people.

Men and women in military gear got out of the jeeps, while ropes fell, and soldiers descended from the helicopters above. They all had rifles and steely looks as they assessed the situation.

Fred pointed at one of the soldiers and gasped. 'The army is here! They're going to save us!'

Lucy shook her head. Not the army.

UNIT.

She recognised the soldiers with their green berets. They were Grandad's people. Yes, Grandad. The kindly old man with the big bushy moustache that used to tell her stories of his days saving the world from alien invaders.

Aliens, and other dangerous forces. Maybe even drop bears.

Was Lieutenant Colonel Hardy here? Coporal Jarrah? Of their scientific advisor Doctor Tahnee Mullina?

But would they remember her, even if they were? How far did Morai's memory wipe go?

Still, it was comforting to know that UNIT were here now, and they might get the situation under control.

Or would they? Lucy remembered the reports of the three-night killing spree in Melbourne from the paper from 2000, so it wasn't going to be easy. But maybe, there was hope.

'Come on!' Fred cried, grabbing her arm, and leading her away with the rest of the crowd as the UNIT soldiers tried to hold the drop bears back.

Several of the creatures attacked, and the UNIT soldiers fired. The rifles didn't contain bullets, but tranquiliser shots. They were putting the drop bears to sleep! Lucy was glad that UNIT weren't killing the drop bears. They were still just animals after all.

In a matter of minutes, UNIT had cordoned off

the street, several drop bears were unconscious on the ground and the others had been driven back. Lucy and Fred watched from a hastily placed barricade as the soldiers marched back and forth, rifles ready, while the helicopters circled the sky above.

She could see more helicopters hovering over the Melbourne skyline. UNIT had clearly deployed all their resources to stop this attack.

There was no sign of Colonel Hardy or Coporal Jarrah. But she did spot Private Larkins, the man that had been pulled through the window by Morai during the attack on the UNIT compound. Fortunately, he had survived that incident.

As Larkins helped move people to safety, Lucy flashed him a smile and a wave. He didn't even react. Perhaps his memories of her were gone after all.

Seeing Larkins and the others in action, Lucy had flashes of memory. UNIT soldiers in the middle of London, cleaning up some alien threat. Grandad's stories about... Yeti in the Underground!

It seemed absurd. But then she was watching Melbourne come under attack from feral koala bears, so maybe it wasn't all so strange, after all?

And then, there was another memory. Her mum, with dark skin like hers, ordering her to wear a dress and arguing over homework. Her dad, with

Caucasian skin like Grandad's. He was reading the newspaper and gave a loud snort of agreement when her mum asked him to support her, without ever looking up from the news article he was reading.

Her friend with the bald head. He wasn't sick. He had something called… alopecia? She remembered his grin and felt one forming on her lips.

The sea. Crisp, clear sea breeze blowing in over a rugged coastline. The remnants of an old castle. And clowns. Why were there clowns? Was this her life?

It was all so overwhelming. These memories, still vague, like snippets of a dream and yet so clear too. Glimpses of her old life. Seeing UNIT in action now, must have triggered those memories.

Just like last time. UNIT was a connection to home.

'Fred!' she gasped, tugging on his sleeve. 'I remember my mum and dad!'

'You do? What are they like?'

Lucy hesitated. 'They're like… I don't know… parents? My mum bosses me around, I think. My dad's more interested in what's going on in the news than what's happening with me.' She paused. It all felt so real. And yet… 'But I miss them, Fred.'

'Of course, you do.'

'I really want to go home.'

'Well, that's not surprising. It's not exactly fun and games here, is it?'

If she wasn't also exhausted and still a little bit scared, she would have laughed. 'I would miss you,' Lucy admitted.

He flashed her a grin. It was very much like the grin her bald friend would give her. Hobo? That was his name. Had he returned from their adventures with Travers and Wells? But there was no time to think about it. Not with the situation she was in now.

She looked at Fred and smiled. 'I'd miss you too.'

Lucy looked down at the time ring on her finger, hoping, maybe for a flash of warmth and light. There was nothing.

The UNIT soldiers began firing tranquiliser darts again as a horde of drop bears began charging towards the barricades. There was a burst of panicked screams from the crowd. In the distance, an explosion sent a plume of smoke into the air. It seemed the drop bears were finally fighting back.

Lucy spotted a group of drop bears climbing up the side of the cinema and jumping across to another building and then another. They were spreading through Melbourne.

There was a panicked scream behind her, and she saw three drop bears jump and attack the edge of the crowd. UNIT soldiers rushed to stop them, but the people had already begun to scatter. Lucy and

Fred were pushed forward and the barricade collapsed to the floor. They had to run to avoid being trampled.

'Where do we go?' Fred cried, as the crowd forced them into a side street away from the cinema and main shops. Behind them, the shouts and rifle shots filled the air. It was terrifying.

Lucy grabbed Fred's hand. 'This way!' she said, leading him away from the mass of people fleeing to safety. They slipped into a dark, smelly alleyway and waited for the crowd to pass.

Aside from the distant glow of a street lamp, it was almost completely pitch black. 'What now?' she asked, unable to hide the nervousness in her voice.

'I have no idea.' Fred sighed. 'If those soldiers can't stop them…'

'We're going to end up with a three-night killing spree, like the papers said,' Lucy replied grimly.

Fred sighed. 'Is it inevitable then?'

Lucy frowned. 'What?'

'The drop bear attack here? The Olympics? What's going to happen if they spread further? What about Australia? The rest of the world? Will the drop bears be contained?'

She shook her head. 'I don't remember ever hearing about drop bears in the rest of the world. Certainly not in the UK. But then, there are still a lot of gaps in my memory.'

'Well, whether they're stopped or not, things are going to get a lot worse,' Fred groaned. 'I just wish I knew what to do to stop them.'

'Well, if UNIT can't hold them back, how can we? What do we have, besides two brooms? I don't think we can do much at all.'

'It's all such a mess, isn't it? We've been missing two days. Drop bears everywhere? What are we going to say, even if they are stopped? How do we explain to my parents, to the police, where we were? I don't think they'd believe us if we we told them we made a quick side trip to the Pliocene era.'

'Or 1895,' Lucy added.

'Or Botany Bay.'

'It's been rather fun though, hasn't it?'

'Dangerous, confusing, but yes it has been fun.'

'I just wish we could sort out this mess.'

With no answers and no real plan, they decided that sitting in an alleyway, close to a massive drop bear attack, was not the safest option. They had no idea if they could get a bus or train out to safety, or just how much of Melbourne was under attack from the drop bears. They didn't even know if Fred's parents were safe. But they couldn't stay here.

They began walking away from the cinema and joined up with a massive crowd of people being evacuated by UNIT soldiers. Helicopters still circled the sky above.

Lucy thought she recognised one of the people stood against a barricade up ahead, dressed in shorts and a large flowery shirt.

'Is that…?' she began.

'Marvin!' Fred exclaimed, loud enough for the owner of Space/Time Books to turn and spot them in the crowd.

Lucy's heart began to race. They hadn't seen him since the discovery of the secret room in the bookstore. She still had so many questions about him. What was he hiding? Why did he seem to know more than he was saying? Why did he take those Polaroids and what was that technology in that back room? It didn't look like it came from 1985.

'There you are!' Marvin cried triumphantly. 'I've been looking for you both everywhere.'

Lucy and Fred looked at each other nervously. Neither knew what to say.

Marvin smiled. 'You can relax, both of you. I know you know about the room in the shop. But I'm not cross.'

He obviously noticed the severity of Lucy's look and held up his arms. 'I mean you no harm.'

'Then why are you looking for us?' Lucy asked suspiciously.

'And what's with that secret room?' Fred demanded. 'What are you hiding? And no lies!'

Marvin's smile dropped, but he still had a glint

in his eye. 'My, so many questions. First, let me reassure you that I am not a bad guy. I genuinely want to help you. I know about the time ring and why it isn't working properly.'

Lucy's eyes narrowed. 'What time ring?'

'That one on your finger?' Marvin said, an eyebrow raised. 'The one that sent you both back and forth through time. I've been trying to track you, but it wasn't easy. I was hoping that each trip would send you back to 1985.'

So, he was lying before? She remembered one more thing. 'You posted the Polaroid to me in 2020?'

Marvin hesitated and then nodded.

'And the words, unfinished business. That was you?'

Marvin licked his lips apprehensively. 'Listen, I'll explain it all to you both as soon as we're safe. First, we need to sort out this drop bear mess.'

'It can be stopped?' Lucy asked cautiously.

Marvin nodded. 'If we can fix the errors in the timeline. I think it all went wrong when you lost the young Thylacoleo Carnifex back in 1894.'

'1895,' Lucy corrected him, before she could stop herself.

'1895, right!'

'You followed us? You can time travel too?' Fred cut in.

'Not exactly. But I can track you. That's what I

do. That room at the back of my shop, that's what it's for. To track disturbances in the timeline.'

'What happened in 1895 after we left?' Lucy asked nervously. 'What happened to the baby Thylacoleo Carnifex?'

'Well, I can't be certain. But I do believe it was a distant, *very* distant relation to the native koala. If I were to hazard a guess, I believe it found other koalas in Australia back in the late nineteenth century and bred with them. Their offspring is what you know as the drop bears.'

'Drop bears are part koala, part Thylacoleo Carnifex?' Fred asked.

Marvin nodded. 'That's right. If you let me help you, I can fix the time ring. We can go back to 1895, find the young Thylacoleo Carnifex, return it to the Pliocene era and restore the timeline.'

Lucy swallowed nervously. 'We have to go back?'

'If you want to save Australia from the rampage of the drop bears? Yes.' Marvin's face grew very serious. 'But we must go now. There are lives at stake! Will you let me help you both?'

Lucy still had questions. Many, many questions. But did she have a choice? She had to trust him. It was the only way.

'Okay, let's do it.'

# CHAPTER TWENTY-FIVE

# ONE LAST MISSION

'Are you sure we can trust him?' Lucy asked Fred as they followed Marvin away from the crowd.

'I don't know.' Fred sighed. 'Before we discovered the room in his shop, I always thought he was kind of quirky but harmless. But I think you were right to agree to his terms. We can't stop the drop bears on our own.'

Lucy nodded. Trusting Marvin was the best chance they had. And if he could help her use the time ring to return home, even better.

'Are you two finished talking about me?' Marvin said, turning around to face them with an encouraging smile. 'I am genuinely here to help.'

'I hope so,' Lucy said defiantly. 'Where are we going?'

'My car is parked nearby. If the drop bears haven't got to it yet. We're going back to my shop.'

'To your secret room?' Fred asked suspiciously.

'My time monitoring lab, you could call it.' Marvin said with a grin. 'Come on. We're close.'

They picked up their pace as they headed onto a deserted street. The UNIT helicopters hovered above them.

Up ahead, they saw a small red car, parked under a tree. Marvin took out his keys from his pocket and opened the front door. He pulled back the front seat and beckoned them inside.

'Are you sure?' Lucy asked Fred.

Fred shrugged. 'I'm as sure as I can be.'

Lucy walked over to the car. Marvin took the brooms from them. 'I'll keep them in the boot. I've got to say, they're interesting weapons.'

'They've proved very effective,' Lucy said, ushering Fred into the back seat before her.

Above them, the branch of the tree began to rustle. 'A drop bear!' Fred cried and looked up just as a twig snapped and leaves fluttered down over their heads.

'Get in!' Marvin cried as a drop bear jumped out of the tree and landed on the roof of the car.

Lucy pushed Fred into the backseat of the car and clambered in after him. Before Marvin could fix the seat and get in himself, a drop bear jumped onto his back and tore at his flowery shirt with its claws.

Marvin screamed. Lucy climbed out and grabbed

one of the brooms that had fallen to the ground. She slammed the flat edge of her *weapon* against the drop bear, and it fell off, stunned. Before it could leap again, she swung the broom, knocking it back further.

A growl filled the air and she turned to see three more drop bears clambering over parked cars towards them. Marvin took the broom from Lucy and swung it threateningly towards the drop bear that had attacked him.

'Get in!' he roared.

Lucy didn't need to be told twice. She climbed into the car and Marvin pushed the front seat back until it clicked. He didn't have time to put the brooms in the boot. He threw it to the ground, climbed in, and slammed the driver door behind him.

The other drop bears attacked. Soon all four were clambering over the vehicle, scratching at the windows to get in. His hand trembling, Marvin put the keys into the ignition and turned. The car engine whirred to life.

'Hold on!' Marvin cried.

The car began to move very fast. Marvin soon picked up enough speed that the drop bears fell off as the car gained momentum. Lucy held on for dear life as she struggled to clasp her seatbelt.

Eventually they were free.

Several police cars and a couple of UNIT jeeps

raced past them as they drove away from the centre of the drop bear attack and made their way across the city towards Space/Time Books.

Lucy didn't know how long the journey lasted. She was exhausted and rested her eyes and she laid her head against the soft leather seat behind her. The lights of Melbourne soared past her as they drove through the night.

Eventually, they reached their destination. Marvin parked the car outside Space/Time Books and got out, wincing a little. His shirt was slashed from where the drop bear had attacked him, and he was obviously injured. But he didn't let it slow him down.

They followed him inside the shop and walked up towards the back room and Marvin's secret time monitoring lab.

Once they were inside the small stock room, Marvin ran his finger down the crack in the paint and the secret door released itself, revealing the mass of multi-coloured lights on the long, thin table. He sat down on the swivel stool and typed something into the computer.

'Okay, I'll be a few minutes. Why don't you both sit down and get some rest. I might have some snacks here somewhere.'

They were too tired to eat. They slumped to the floor, resting their backs against a wall, and waited for Marvin to do what he needed to do.

Marvin sniffed. 'What *is* that smell?'

'Vegemite,' Fred replied with a half-yawn.

'Vegemite? What on earth…'

'To keep the drop bears away.'

Marvin chuckled. 'The three rules! How did that work out for you? Did you call them Bruce?'

Lucy and Fred looked at each other but said nothing. It all felt rather foolish now.

'I'll get you some clean clothes and soap to wash up,' Marvin said, rising from his seat. 'The system will take a few minutes to run all the computations.'

Lucy didn't really have any idea what Marvin was talking about, but any excuse to wipe the Vegemite off her face, arms and legs would be most welcome. He soon returned with hot water, soap, and towels to allow them both to clean up.

She was certain they probably stank of more than just Vegemite. It had been a long, long time since she had a shower. Between the settler's camp at Botany Bay and nineteenth century Melbourne, their destinations hadn't exactly been the cleanest of places.

Marvin also gave them a change of clothes each. Lucy didn't know why he had t-shirts and shorts that fitted them, but she didn't question it. Their clothes were embedded with two days of sand, dirt and sweat.

When they were done, Marvin ushered them to join him around his chair.

'Right, one last mission. I've calculated the exact spot you lost the Thylacoleo Carnifex in 1895. If we can program the time ring exactly, we can get there, pick it up and drop in back in the year One Million and 90 BC.'

Lucy's jaw dropped. 'We went to the year One Million and 90 BC?'

Marvin grinned. 'That time ring really can take you places.' He typed something back into the computer. 'We can check back into the year 2000, make sure the Olympics go off uninterrupted, and then be back here in time for tea. Sound like a plan?'

'How does the time ring work?' Lucy asked nervously.

'It's attuned to your thought patterns, but it runs on a Zeta-Beltar wave that taps into the space, time…' Marvin paused. 'But you don't need to know all that.'

'Yes we do!' Fred exclaimed.

Marvin laughed. 'Perhaps I'll go into the science once we get back.'

'I think that's best,' Lucy replied, much to Fred's disappointment. 'Are you sure it's working properly? I've not been able to control it correctly.'

'Hmmm,' Marvin said, rubbing his chin. 'Let me check. Hold out your hand. Let me see the ring.'

Lucy held out the hand with the ring nervously, while Marvin grabbed a small device from the table that looked like… a mobile phone. Lucy wasn't sure how she'd forgotten about mobile phones when everyone in her time seemed to have one glued to their hand! Lucy was starting to get a small headache from all the things she had remembered over the last half an hour or so.

A green glow erupted from the end of the device, giving out a soft whirring noise as he hovered it over the ring.

'Ah, I see. The Theta-Alpha Roitar is damaged. It's flinging you all over time with no real safety barriers. I'm surprised you weren't scatted into a million pieces.'

Lucy gave Fred a look of alarm. She didn't like the sound of that.

Marvin chuckled. 'Relax! I made it sound worse than it was. Let me fix it.' He pressed another button on the device and a blue light flickered several times. 'Good, that should do it.'

'So, what do I do?'

'Hold on!' Marvin left the room and return with a cage with what looked like a small, electronic lock. 'We'll need this to capture the young Thylacoleo Carnifex.'

He looked at them both, strapping the device he had used to fix the time ring to his belt. 'The worst is over. If we are lucky, the whole trip back and forth through time should take less than an hour. Are you both ready?'

'I guess so,' Lucy said, apprehensively.

'Ready,' Fred said with a nod.

Marvin nodded too. 'Good. Now everyone, hold on to Lucy. And Lucy, this should be much easier given that you've been to these places before. I want you to think about the last place you were in 1895. Can you do that?'

Lucy nodded.

'Good. Now concentrate hard and the ring should do the rest.'

Lucy took a deep breath as Fred and Marvin put their hands on her shoulders. 'Let's go.'

The room vanished in a flash of white light around her.

# CHAPTER TWENTY-SIX

# BACK TO THE PAST

The docks of nineteenth century Melbourne appeared around them. Lucy could smell the mix of sea air and sewage almost immediately. It was worse than the Vegemite.

Still, it was thrilling to be back in the past again, looking at the big ships with their masts and sails, like something out of an old movie. This time, she could afford the time to take in the view.

Marvin let out a low whistle. 'Wow, this is something else.'

Fred looked at him suspiciously. 'Have you travelled in time before, Marvin?'

'We'll, I've never been to 1895 before.'

Lucy noted that he hadn't answered the question. Was he really from the 1980s? Was he really from Australia?

Marvin had a look of excitement, as he took the strange device from his belt. 'Let's see if we can find the young Thylacoleo Carnifex before it escapes completely.'

'Are you certain we're at the same time and place we were before?' Fred asked.

Lucy noticed one ship with a torn pale blue sail that was being mended by two men in white shirts. They were high up on the rigging and didn't seem to be paying them any attention.

'I think that ship was here before,' she told them.

'Good,' Marvin nodded. 'Visible landmarks are good. Anything else you recognise?'

'Well, I don't see any members of that Gilded Serpent Society anywhere.' Fred observed.

Marvin frowned. 'The what?'

'Oh, you know… just some nineteenth century gangsters. At least I think they were gangsters.'

Lucy wondered if the ship with Alistair and the other men was still at the docks. There was a gap where she thought it had been berthed. On the horizon, she could make out one ship, sailing away from Melbourne.

She assumed they were gone. It was almost disappointing. If that had been her great, great grandfather she would have loved to have spoken to him more.

Was he just like Grandad? The one thing she knew for certain was that he was a hero. Lucy guessed it ran in the family.

'Got it!' Marvin cried, waving the device around excitedly. 'Follow me!'

They ran behind Marvin as he hurried, huffing, and puffing down one of the paths created between the rows and rows of boxes and crates. Lucy was reminded just how exhausted she was.

'This way!' Marvin said, turning left sharply and taking another path through the crates. Lucy and Fred followed him out into an open square beyond the crates, much like the one that they had tried to catch the creature in the last time they had been here.

Something darted across the square, leaping off a crate. It was the baby Thylacoleo Carnifex!

'My, that's fast!' Marvin exclaimed. 'We can't have that.'

Marvin flicked a switch on the device and a wide beam of light blazed out on the path just ahead of the creature. The moment it ran into the light, the Thylacoleo Carnifex froze.

'What was that?' Fred asked in wonder.

Lucy didn't know what to think. Who was this man with his strange contraptions, time monitoring rooms and knowledge of time travel? She had a million questions for him, but she would have to wait until this mess was fixed.

'Is it… okay?' she asked hesitantly. As dangerous as the baby Thylacoleo Carnifex was, it wasn't intentionally evil. She didn't want any harm to come to it if she could help it.

'It's asleep,' Marvin replied, opening the lock on the cage he was carrying. Carefully, he picked up the docile creature and placed it inside. It began to stir as he reactivated the lock, letting out a low, rumbling growl.

'What now?' Fred asked.

Marvin turned to Lucy. 'That's up to you. Are you ready to take us back to the year One Million and 90 BC?'

Lucy looked at the ring nervously. 'I think so.'

'Good,' Marvin said, attaching the device to his belt, picking up the cage with the baby Thylacoleo Carnifex inside and putting his free hand on her shoulder. Fred put his hand on her other shoulder.

'So, do I just remember where we were last?' Lucy asked.

Marvin nodded. 'Yes. Picture the scenery, the smells, the heat, anything else you can muster. The time ring will lock onto that memory and pull you back there.'

'Perhaps we could arrive outside the cave?' Fred suggested.

Lucy shuddered. The last thing they wanted was to arrive in the middle of the Thylacoleo Carnifex nest and be eaten before they could release the baby.

'I'll do my best,' she said nervously and concentrated on the memory of the rocky landscape outside the cave, with the small stream that ran into the wall of rock. The smell of dust in the air, the heat of the beating sun…

…in a flash of white light, the docks of nineteenth century Melbourne vanished and they found themselves back in the Pleistocene period. It was as hot as she remembered. Hotter perhaps. She immediately felt the burning heat of the sun above them.

'Wow, this is worse than the beach in a heatwave!' Marvin exclaimed, setting the cage down on the ground.

Lucy immediately spotted the stream that ran under the small opening into the Thylacoleo Carnifex cave beyond. Hopefully, this was the right place. It felt hot enough to be the right place.

'I'm confused,' Fred began, wiping sweat from his brow. 'You said the baby Thylacoleo Carnifex mated with a koala and bred a drop bear. What about the Thylacoleo Carnifex itself? I've seen a full-size one. Wouldn't someone have spotted it in all these years?'

'I did see a newspaper report from the end of the nineteenth century,' Marvin replied. 'Several hunters were killed outside Melbourne in 1897, tracking a lion. Most people put it down to a hoax, but maybe it was your creature, all grown up. They apparently caught and killed it, so I assume it didn't cause too much damage on its own.'

'That's lucky, I guess. I've seen a full-size Thylacoleo Carnifex. They're pretty deadly.'

'Like that?' Marvin gasped, pointing out at the rocks above.

Lucy looked up in horror as three adult Thylacoleo Carnifexes appeared on a rocky ledge above, fangs bared, their beady eyes glinting in the sun as they took in their prey. She had forgotten just how terrifying they were.

Marvin scrambled to open the electronic lock on the cage, as the three Thylacoleo Carnifexes scrambled down the rocks towards them. The baby Thylacoleo Carnifex crawled out slowly. Lucy wasn't sure if it was still sluggish from the effects of the device Marvin had used, or if it was genuinely scared.

As soon as the baby was free, Marvin grabbed the cage and ran back towards Lucy. She screamed as the three adult Thylacoleo Carnifexes closed in around them. Behind her, Fred clutched her shoulder trembling.

'Get us out of here!' he yelled.

'Where?'

'We should go to the year 2000!' Marvin yelled. 'Check that everything is okay. But be quick!'

He grabbed her shoulder tightly. Lucy looked at the ring and concentrated as hard as she could as the first of the Thylacoleo Carnifex began to leap towards them, claws ready.

Its paw was just inches from her face, when a white light filled the air around them, carrying Lucy, Marvin and Fred away from the Pleistocene period…

…and into the harsh light of the Sydney Olympic Stadium.

They were stood in the almost empty foyer. There were a few people working behind the food stands, but the sounds of cheering coming from within the centre of the stadium was almost deafening.

Marvin, Lucy and Fred looked at each other hesitantly, taking in their surroundings. No one seemed to have noticed their sudden appearance out of thin air.

'That doesn't sound like screaming,' Fred said.

'I agree,' Lucy replied with a nod. 'But we should check it out. The drop bears might not have attacked yet.'

'Lead the way,' Marvin said. He laid the cage down under a bench out of sight and they quickly approached the nearest door to the stadium seating. They were greeted by the same ticket attendant as before.

'Tickets please.' She didn't seem to recognise them.

Marvin stepped forward. 'Hi, yeah. My wife's got them. She's seated down there,' he said, pointing to no particular person in the crowd of seated people. 'My son, he desperately needed the loo. I forgot to grab the tickets when we came back up.'

'Hmmm,' the ticket inspector mumbled. 'Well, you need to make sure you have them at all times.'

'I will, sorry,' Marvin said with a broad smile.

'Okay, off you go then.'

They stepped through into the packed seating area. In the stadium below, Lucy saw the multi-coloured dressed brass band begin to play. She remembered this well. In a moment, a voice would announce the arrival the Governor-General of Australia and the President of the International Olympic Committee.

And then, the drop bears would attack.

She also noticed the woman with the pink hair sat near the front of the tier, with empty seats either side of her.

Lucy held her breath, waiting for the music to play, watching the faces of the crowds cheering and smiling in the stands, unaware of the drop bear attack that might come any moment. She remembered that Fred and her had been so caught up in enjoying the opening ceremony, that they had been completely unprepared for the attack.

She wouldn't be unprepared this time.

The music ended, the same French man's voice echoed over the speakers and there was a white light like last time, lighting up a section of the seating.

'Ladies and gentlemen. Will you please welcome his excellency, the honourable Sir William Deane, the Governor-General of Australia, and the President of the International Olympic Committee Juan Antonio Samaranch.'

This was it. The moment of truth. The trumpets rang out and one of the two men in the lit-up seating area waved to the crowd…

…No attack came. The trumpets continue to be played. The cheers from the crowd filled the stadium and the opening games continued.

After a few minutes, Lucy turned to Fred and Marvin. 'I guess it worked.'

Fred grinned. 'Not a single drop bear in sight.'

Lucy looked at Marvin anxiously. 'Thank you.'

'No, thank you,' he said with a smile. 'It's your courage that helped take us back and fix the timeline. Shall we go back home?'

Fred frowned. 'Is 1985 your home, really?'

'Of course,' Marvin said. 'Where else would I be?'

That sounded like another ambiguous answer. She would allow him this one. As soon as they got back to 1985, she wanted the truth.

They returned to the main foyer, getting a few odd looks from the ticket attendant, and picked up the cage from under the bench.

Fred picked up a newspaper that someone had

discarded.

'It's the same one I bought in Sydney,' he said, retrieving his copy from his backpack. They scanned the headlines. Most of the content was the same, but there was no mention of any drop bear attack or an historic three-night killing spree in Melbourne in 1985.

'I think we can take this as confirmation that the mission worked,' Fred said triumphantly.

Lucy let out a deep breath of relief. 'No more drop bears. I won't be sad to see them go.'

'Well, I certainly won't look at koalas the same way again,' Fred added.

'Shall we head back to 1985?' Marvin suggested. 'Though, let's find somewhere a little more out of sight to disappear.'

'Agreed,' Lucy said, leading them behind a food stand, out of sight of the main walkway. The stand was unmanned and there was no one about that would spot them.

Marvin put his hand gently on her shoulder, Fred the other and she looked down at the time ring one more time, concentrating on the secret back room in Marvin's store.

There was a flash of white light and they left, letting the 2000 Olympics continue, without any drop bears to hinder it.

# EPILOGUE

They were back in Space/Time Books. But not quite as it was when they last saw it. It was daylight outside, and they soon discovered that they had arrived just after the moment they had first discovered Marvin's secret room two days earlier.

Before the trip back to the night Matty arrived in Australia, before the museum, the journey back to the Pleistocene era, the Thylacoleo Carnifex, 1895, Botany Bay and the night the drop bears attacked.

It also meant that Fred didn't have to explain to his parents where he had been gone for the last two days.

Marvin, somehow, wasn't in two places at once. Like them, he remembered everything about the drop bear attack in Melbourne and the mission through time to fix it. He didn't really explain how he could take the place of his earlier self, but there were bigger questions that needed answering.

Marvin walked up the stairs to where they were sat, resting by rows and rows of new books. He was carrying a tray of mugs filled with steaming hot tea, which he placed on the floor next to them. Lucy took a mug eagerly. She needed the energy.

Marvin sat down, cross-legged beside them, watching them.

Lucy took a few sips of the tea and then turned her attention to the mysterious bookshop owner.

'Okay, can I have some answers now?'

Marvin nodded. 'Absolutely, Miss Wilson. I'm sure you have many, many questions. But first let me answer one. Let me tell you why I really brought you here to 1985...'